ROBOT RACERS
BOOK #3

Robot Racers is published in the United States by
Stone Arch Books, A Capstone Imprint
1710 Roe Crest Drive
North Mankato, Minnesota 56003
www.capstonepub.com

First published in 2013 by Curious Fox,
an imprint of Capstone Global Library Limited
7 Pilgrim Street, London, EC4V 6LB
Registered company number: 6695582
www.curious-fox.com

Library of Congress Cataloging-in-Publication Data is available on the Library
of Congress website.

ISBN: 978-1-4342-6572-2 (hardcover)
ISBN: 978-1-4342-7938-5 (paperback)

Summary: After surviving the canyon and jungle stages of the Robot Races,
the racers are whisked off to the Arctic, where not everyone is playing fair.
Will Horace and Zoom put Jimmy and Maverick's chances of winning on ice?

Artistic Elements: Shutterstock

Designer: Alison Thiele

With special thanks to David Grant

Printed in China.
092013   007740LEO

ROBOT RACERS
ARCTIC ADVENTURE

BY AXEL LEWIS

MADISON PUBLIC LIBRARY
Madison, South Dakota

STONE ARCH BOOKS™
a capstone imprint www.capstonepub.com

TABLE OF CONTENTS

CHAPTER 1
DESTINATION UNKNOWN

The huge steel door of the airship clanged shut. The airlock sealed it with a hiss and a thud. The robot racers were on their way.

Jimmy Roberts hurried to one of the tiny portholes. He headed past the workstations where the racers' teams were working like crazy on their state-of-the-art robots. Jimmy's own robot, Maverick, was already updated. Jimmy's grandpa, Wilfred Roberts, sat next to Maverick, enjoying a celebratory cup of tea.

By the time Jimmy got to the little round window, they were way above the ground. He peered down from the airship at his little house.

He could just about make out the garden shed where Grandpa had built Maverick out of a rusty old taxicab and scrap material.

It had been almost two months since Lord Leadpipe had announced that he would be opening up his world-famous racing championship to children for the first time.

In a whirlwind few days, Jimmy had learned that his jolly old grandpa was actually a genius robot inventor who used to work for the most secret department of the Secret Services. Grandpa had built Maverick for Jimmy so that he could compete in the Robot Races against some of the best robots in the world.

And now here they were, on their way to the third stage of the competition.

Jimmy could hardly believe he was a robot racer, no matter how many times he thought about it. Even when he said it out loud.

The house and garden shed got smaller and smaller as the airship climbed higher, until Jimmy's hometown of Smedingham was so far away that it looked like a toy town. The cars driving along the busy streets seemed to crawl over them like tiny bugs. And then they were high in the clouds, and Jimmy couldn't see anything at all.

"Hey, Jimmy!"

Jimmy turned to see Sammy walking toward him. Sammy was one of the other competitors and Jimmy's new friend. He was from Egypt.

Jimmy grinned and gave his friend a high five. "Hey, Sammy, how's it going?"

"Good, thank you," said Sammy in his strong North African accent. "And how are you? Have you recovered from our adventure in the jungle?"

"I think so," said Jimmy with a smile. "And I'm ready for another one."

"In the jungle?" asked Sammy.

"Wherever we're going," said Jimmy.

Jimmy, Sammy, and the other robot racers had competed in the depths of a South American jungle in their last race. The track had introduced them to scary creatures, lakes of quicksand, and even an ancient temple.

Jimmy noticed Sammy looking over his shoulder at Maverick, his eyebrows lifting in surprise. Jimmy figured his friend was checking Maverick out, looking for any modifications or new gadgets.

While Sammy was busy looking at Maverick, Jimmy snatched a glance over Sammy's shoulder to see what changes had been made to his robot, Maximus, since the jungle race. The huge hoverbot looked just the same, although it was a lot cleaner now that the jungle mud and swamp splats had been washed off. Maybe the enormous propellers that powered the hoverbot were slightly larger than before. And what was that new door on the front? Was it hiding some amazing new gadget?

"You have been practicing your driving?" asked Sammy.

"Well . . ." said Jimmy. He didn't want to say that he had driven Maverick just once since he and Sammy had roared to a shared victory in the Rain Forest Rampage leg of the championship. But there just weren't that many places in his hometown of Smedingham where a kid could take a rocket-powered robot for a spin.

Jimmy's one test drive around the back streets of his neighborhood had ended with a neighbor's garden fence on fire and some nasty burn marks on their patio umbrella, thanks to his upgraded rocket-boosters. Jimmy grimaced at the thought.

Luckily the firefighters had arrived quickly. And while they were there, they had rescued the neighbor's terrified cat that had run up a tree and refused to come down. Grandpa and Jimmy had agreed he should lay off the driving practice for a while.

As Jimmy and Sammy talked, all the other competitors came wandering over. There was Princess Kako from Japan, wearing her signature silver leather. Her hair was slicked back and tied in a neat bun. She was straight-faced and silent as usual.

Beside her, Chip, an African-American boy, strode along in his usual T-shirt, jeans, and baseball cap. He was chatting to Missy, the loud

Australian, who was shouting back at him at her usual deafening volume. Her wild red curls hung loose around her shoulders, and Jimmy could see the usual grease smears on her blue jeans and face, showing the hard work she had been doing to improve her robot racer, Monster.

"Hey, Jimmy!" she bellowed. "How's it going?" She thumped Jimmy on the back so hard he stopped breathing for a few seconds.

"Fine," wheezed Jimmy. "Thanks for asking. How are you?"

"Couldn't be better, mate!" yelled Missy, thumping him again.

Jimmy tried to speak but ended up just nodding.

"Good to see you all again," Chip said. He beamed, looking around at the group of drivers. "Hey! Where did Horace go?"

A sudden blast from Maverick's horn made them all turn sharply. They spun around to see Horace jumping away from Maverick. He had blond hair and tanned skin from all the holidays he went on with his wealthy parents, and perfectly straight white teeth that he used to pull a smug grin whenever he had the chance.

Jimmy and Horace had gone to school together back in Smedingham, but they had never been friends.

"Ha!" Horace laughed nervously, trying to pretend he hadn't been spying on someone else's robot. "What a charming horn that is."

He strolled back to where the other drivers stood. "Hello again, Jimmy." He grinned, his white teeth gleaming. "Maverick's looking like he's ready for the junkyard, as usual."

"Had a good look, huh, Horace?" asked Jimmy.

"There wasn't much to see," said Horace, sneering.

"So where do you think we will be racing this time?" asked Sammy, interrupting them before they could argue any further.

"No idea," said Jimmy, turning his attention back to the others.

"I am hoping for some sand," Sammy said and smiled. "A nice desert, perhaps."

"Or a beach in the Caribbean!" suggested Chip. "Miles of white sand, clear blue sea . . ."

"I'd like a big city," said Princess Kako. "Smooth, wide city streets are much better than the dark and mud of the jungle. And also the shops and restaurants and hotels . . ." she added with a faraway look in her eyes. "Yes. The city is where we should go."

"Don't be soft!" bellowed Missy, rubbing her hands together excitedly. "I want somewhere a little more exciting than that. Up a volcano or down a mineshaft or —"

"Yes!" said Jimmy, his brain fizzing with excitement. "Or through some underground caves. Or over the Himalayas!"

"What about you, Horace?" asked Chip. "What do you want?"

"Zoom can cope with any terrain," Horace said, a sneer on his face once again. "And my NASA engineers are prepared for anything. So unlike you losers, I don't really care."

"As long as there isn't any quicksand, eh, Horace?" said Missy, giggling.

The others burst out laughing, remembering how Horace had found himself in a sticky situation during their last race.

Horace didn't join in with the laughter. He narrowed his eyes and gritted his shiny teeth. Jimmy couldn't help but think that the Australian girl would pay for that comment. Horace was definitely one competitor who knew how to hold a grudge.

"Hey, Jimmy," said Sammy, "maybe we will have another adventure together like last time." He laughed. "But I am hoping not. I think this race would be better if we don't see so many snakes, no?"

"I thought we were going to spend the rest of our lives stuck in that temple," replied Jimmy.

"And the rest of our lives would not have lasted a long time," said Sammy. "When you are in a booby-trapped temple and the walls are trying to squash you, it is not so good for your health."

"All right, all right, you two," shrieked Missy, cutting Sammy off with a playful nudge in the ribs. "We had to listen to this all the way back from the jungle. Don't make us hear it all over again! We know you're Sammy's biggest fan, Jimmy, and Sammy thinks you're the best. But remember, we're all competing against each other here."

"Don't worry," said Jimmy. "You'll all be eating my dust in the next race."

"I think not," replied Sammy. "I will be winning the next race."

As the rest of the group continued to chatter, Jimmy began to feel a thrill shooting up his spine at the thought of the next race. This entire race was such a dream come true for him! But then Jimmy remembered what Grandpa had said as they were waiting for Lord Leadpipe's airship to come and get them.

"You're in first place on the leaderboard, but there are four more races to be run," Grandpa had said, his white mustache bouncing up and down over his top lip. "And goodness only knows what ridiculous nonsense that old fool Lord Loonpipe has got rattling around in his tiny brain. He could have planned anything for this next race, so keep your head up and one eye on your rearview mirror." And then he gave Jimmy a big hug.

The smile slowly faded from Jimmy's lips, and instead he felt a jolt of fear squirming in his belly. Now as he looked around at the other competitors, he started to worry.

What if I'm not prepared? What if Maverick can't handle the conditions? Lord Leadpipe could have planned anything.

A cold sweat spread up Jimmy's back, and his stomach climbed into his throat. Then his ears started popping.

Jimmy realized that it wasn't fear sending his stomach somersaulting around his body. It was the airship descending.

"We're landing!" shouted Chip.

The racers rushed over to one of the little round portholes around the edge of the airship's enormous hangar and peered out.

"I can't see a thing," shrieked Missy.

"Me neither," said Sammy.

Jimmy stared out into the whiteness of solid cloud as the airship shuddered. There was a thud beneath Jimmy's feet, which made him jump.

"I think we've landed," said Chip.

"Nah," said Missy, "I can still see clouds. We're still in the air, for sure."

Jimmy pressed his face up against the window and tried to peer out, but his breath kept fogging up the glass. All he could see was blank white space.

Why can't I see anything? Jimmy thought. *This is beyond strange.*

"Maybe we've landed on top of a mountain," cried Chip. "A mountain so high that we're racing up in the clouds!"

"Perhaps Lord Leadpipe's built a track in the sky!" cried Sammy.

"You idiots!" Horace yelled.

"So where are we then, Mr. Clever Pants?" snapped Missy.

Horace was just about to reply when a creaking sound — a loud, metallic groan — interrupted him.

The huge steel door of the airship shook. All six competitors stood and stared open-mouthed as the crack of daylight at the top of the door began to grow.

"I think we're about to find out," said Jimmy.

CHAPTER 2
SURPRISES

Jimmy stared, wide-eyed, as the huge steel door of the airship was lowered on its huge steel hinges. He narrowed his eyes as the crack of white light got wider and brighter.

Then a blast of freezing air hit him in the face and a flurry of white specks flew in, coating his eyebrows and hair in a fine white frost. Jimmy flinched, wiping the flakes out of his eyes. He peered again through the huge airship doorway into the whiteness. He couldn't believe what he was seeing.

It's not clouds, he thought. *It's snow! Miles and miles of snow.*

As his eyes became more accustomed to the dazzling glare coming from beyond the hangar doors, he could see the white surface more clearly as it stretched off to the horizon in every direction.

Even the clanging and banging and shouting of the team mechanics stopped as they all put down their tools and came to stare out at the scene.

Another sudden sharp gust of freezing air whipped through the doorway, sending a pile of paper blueprints flying through the air and knocking a stack of empty oil cans to the ground. Behind him, Jimmy could hear angry voices cursing, followed by several mechanics scurrying to clean up the mess. The poster that Jimmy's team sponsor, That's Shallot!, had pinned to his workstation wall was ripped loose. It fluttered around among the tools for a second before another gust whisked it outside through the doorway.

Jimmy gasped at the cold as the howling wind hurled snow in every direction. His teeth began to chatter, and he wished he had been wearing a coat.

"Look!" said Chip, pointing to some object in the distance.

As the wind dropped, the snow thinned slightly, and Jimmy could just make out the shape of a white dome against the gray sky.

"It's an igloo!" shrieked Missy. "A huge igloo!"

"And look!" Sammy gasped.

A figure was emerging from the little tunnel at the front of the igloo, slowly squeezing its way out into the frozen landscape. The person stopped for a moment and looked around, then headed straight for the airship, stomping along in heavy brown boots and a huge, furry hooded coat.

"Anyone speak Eskimo?" asked Missy.

"I think it's called Inuit," said Chip. "And, no. Not a word. Whaddya think he wants?"

"Maybe he wants to know why someone's parked an enormous airship next to his house," said Princess Kako.

"I think he's angry," said Horace. He crouched down behind Jimmy, his teeth chattering. "He's getting closer!"

Horace was right. The figure was coming straight toward them. It even raised a hand and waved at them. Then it slowly pulled back its hood to reveal a man wearing a monocle, which glinted in the light from the blinding white snow. It was Lord Ludwick Leadpipe!

"Greetings, competitors!" he shouted over the noise of the wind. "Welcome to the Arctic Circle. If you would like to get into your racers and join me out on the snow, I'll tell you all about the next leg of the competition."

It took a moment for this to sink in. The competitors turned to each other, grinning in amazement, before hurrying off to their robots.

"We're in the Arctic!" said Jimmy as he hopped into Maverick's cockpit.

"I-I-I-I-know!" stammered Maverick, his pistons spluttering in the subzero temperature.

"You'll warm up soon," said Jimmy, wondering if his teeth were chattering from the cold or from excitement. It was really hard to tell at this point.

The pit area echoed with the sound of engines roaring as the racers fired up their robots and prepared to head out onto the ice.

Jimmy and Maverick were out first. They eased out of their workstation and made their way toward the doorway. A thick layer of snow was already gathering on the ground. They edged slowly onto the steep ramp, but Maverick immediately began to slide. Jimmy stomped on the brakes, but it didn't stop them from sliding down the slope.

"Whoaaaa," shuddered Maverick, skidding out across the ice and spinning to a stop.

"Uh, I think we're going to need some different tires," said Jimmy, trying to stay calm.

He watched the other racers follow them down the ramp from the huge airship. Missy and Monster shot off the ramp onto the slippery ground, Monster's huge tires spinning and spraying snow everywhere while Missy howled with laughter.

Next came Chip and Dug, moving slowly but surely, his caterpillar tracks gripping the ice with ease. Sammy and his hoverbot, Maximus, sat nervously at the top of the ramp for a moment before gliding smoothly over the ice and coming to a controlled stop next to Maverick and Jimmy.

Princess Kako and her robobike, Lightning, followed very slowly and carefully. Kako added extra stability by stabbing the sharp points of her heavy biker boots into the ice.

Lastly Horace and Zoom rocketed down the ramp and across the ice. They screeched to a dramatic stop as Horace pulled an emergency-brake turn.

"This ice is no problem for the tires my NASA team has developed!" he shouted.

Soon all the parents and mechanics joined the racers, wrapped up in padded coats, boots, scarves, gloves, and fur hats. Herding them like a sheepdog was Joshua Johnson, the robot coordinator. He was dressed like a yeti in a brown, furry jacket, brown furry pants, and big furry boots. Joshua's huge smile looked even bigger than usual. Jimmy couldn't help but wonder if it had been frozen into position.

Jimmy waved at Grandpa. At least, he thought it was Grandpa — it looked like his mustache poking out of the fur-lined hood.

Grandpa came over, and Jimmy opened Maverick's window.

"You look cozy, Grandpa," Jimmy said, smiling.

"Typical Loonpipe!" mumbled Grandpa through his furry hood. "He has to put on a show. Why can't he just hold the race on a normal racetrack?"

"Drivers," announced Joshua Johnson through a megaphone, "please exit your vehicles for your race briefing."

Jimmy got out of Maverick and shivered. Grandpa handed him a thick, furry coat and Jimmy quickly wrapped himself up in it.

"Attention, please!" called Lord Leadpipe's voice.

Jimmy and Grandpa looked around to see where the voice was coming from.

"Look!" said Jimmy. He pointed to where Lord Leadpipe was standing on a massive block of ice with a microphone in his hand. He was surrounded by camerabots who had appeared from another section of the huge airship.

"Here we go again," mumbled Grandpa.

"Racers," continued Lord Leadpipe, "welcome to the Arctic stage of the Robot Races Championship! There are three — yes, three! — different tracks that you can choose to follow in this race."

The competitors all shifted nervously from one foot to another at this unexpected surprise.

"There will be no pit stops on any of the three tracks, so you should choose carefully," warned Lord Leadpipe, wagging a warning finger of his fur glove at the competitors. "And play to your strengths. The first route you can choose," he continued, a grin spreading across his face, "will take you over the Arctic Ocean, navigating your way through the narrow channels between the huge ice cliffs. Fall in, and you will face the dark, cold depths of the sea."

Jimmy swallowed hard and tried not to shiver.

"The second route," said Lord Leadpipe, "is on land over the snowy terrain of Greenland. Should you choose this route, you will need to be constantly on the lookout for snow-covered crevasses. These huge cracks in the Earth's surface can be up to half a mile deep. Not to mention the howling, freezing winds stirring up snowstorms that can cause you to lose your way in the blink of an eye."

"None of them sound too appealing so far," whispered Grandpa.

"And the third route," continued Lord Leadpipe, "will take you across the frozen sheets of ice covering the sea. The ice could give way at any moment," he added. "And I hardly need to mention that on all three routes there is the possibility of hypothermia, snow blindness, and frostbite — after all, it is a little chilly out here, isn't it?"

"Sounds like it's going to be a barrel of laughs from start to finish," Maverick joked.

Lightning, meanwhile, was showing off. In a blur of flying snow and flashing black metal, his wheels folded in and he transformed into a sled and then back to robobike again.

Monster responded by raising his front grille and pushing out a massive snowplow that looked like it could clear an iceberg. At the controls, Missy grinned proudly.

Chip's robot racer, Dug, raised his crane arm and swung it in a circle over their heads. He brought it down with an almighty crash on the ice, sending a three-foot-wide crack ripping through the ice.

"We have some work to do if we're going to win this one, Maverick!" said Jimmy, giving his robot an affectionate pat on the hood.

"I'm processing my software already," said Maverick, his computers whirring away somewhere behind his dashboard.

"You have just one day to prepare for the race," said Lord Leadpipe. "But in the meantime, I have a couple of surprises for you," he said. "The first is this; the winner of tomorrow's race will not only receive ten points to add to their score on the leader board, but he or she will also be presented with a very special prize from Leadpipe Industries."

"I bet it's some kind of upgrade," said Jimmy, his eyes glistening with excitement. "A top-of-the-range upgrade ——"

"— which will be mine when I beat you losers by miles," said Horace, appearing suddenly at Jimmy's shoulder.

"We'll see about that," muttered Jimmy, grinding his teeth.

"Not that I need any upgrades, of course." Horace continued, more smugly than ever. "Zoom is already fully top-of-the-range from top to bottom."

"And the other surprise . . ." said Lord Leadpipe, "will be revealed later on."

And with a final wink to the contestants, he leaped down from his ice block and strolled back to the igloo.

CHAPTER 3
THREE'S A TEAM

Jimmy ran to get into Maverick. Grandpa followed and climbed into the passenger's seat as Jimmy fired up the robot's engine.

"Can you believe it, Grandpa?" said Jimmy, brimming with excitement as they cruised back up the ramp and into Maverick's workstation. "There's a special prize for winning this race. A Leadpipe Industries upgrade, I bet."

"Yes, yes," said Grandpa, showing no interest at all as Jimmy parked and secured the emergency brake. "I don't think we'll be needing any of their garbage, thank you very much," he continued. "Although I could probably get something useful out of it. Something to make the auto-vacuum get around the carpet a little quicker, perhaps . . ."

"Don't worry, Maverick," came Horace's voice echoing across the airship. "I don't think there are any snakes in the Arctic, so you won't need to spend half the race screaming like a baby. You know, like you did in the rain forest." Horace's head popped up from behind Zoom, and he threw his head back and laughed.

"You'll be the one screaming like a baby when we win, Horace!" Jimmy shouted back.

"You tell him, Jimmy," said Maverick. "We'll show him what Jimmy Roberts and Maverick are made of!"

"Yeah?" Horace called back.

"Yeah!" shouted Maverick, shaking so much that Jimmy thought he might blow a gasket. "Who's first on the championship leaderboard? Me and Jimmy! Where did you and Zoom place in the Rain Forest Rampage, huh?"

Horace opened and closed his mouth like a fish out of water, but he couldn't think of a good response. Instead he stomped his foot with a thud and disappeared into the crowd of NASA engineers surrounding Zoom.

Jimmy bit his lip and clenched his fists. He hated arguing. But try as he might, he couldn't stop Horace from getting under his skin. Just the thought of watching his smug face at the top of the podium made Jimmy feel a surge of competitiveness.

"There's no way we're going to let them beat us," Jimmy muttered.

"It's not all about winning, you know, my boy," whispered Grandpa, resting a comforting hand on Jimmy's shoulder. "You just do your best, and I'll be proud of you."

"What's all this shouting?" came Lord Leadpipe's voice. "A little friendly banter — a dash of the competitive spirit! That's the ticket, racers. Good to see some passion and fire in your bellies. That's what this competition needs."

"Now hold on a minute, Leadpipe," said Grandpa, stepping in front of Jimmy as though to protect him. "I don't need you encouraging my grandson to act like that! What kind of a role model do you think you are?"

Lord Leadpipe frowned, like he was struggling to work out a complex calculation in his head. "I say, Wilfred, I don't quite know what you're talking about —"

"Never mind pretending you're all innocent," Grandpa continued, ignoring the billionaire's protests. "You wander around in that ridiculous furry outfit, looking like a stuffed grizzly bear. You drag us to the ends of the Earth with no warning at all. In fact, I haven't even brought a pair of woolly winter socks. What do you think this cold is going to do to my poor circulation?"

"I —" Lord Leadpipe tried to say, but there was no stopping Grandpa.

"Do you know what the temperature is out there? I think you could have warned us that you were —"

"I —" Lord Leadpipe tried again.

"Grandpa!" Jimmy tried to interrupt.

"— landing us in the middle of a blizzard,"

continued Grandpa. "It's completely irresponsible to bring children to a dangerous place like this and expect them to —"

"Grandpa!" bellowed Jimmy.

Finally Grandpa fell silent, his red cheeks puffing plumes of fog into the icy air.

"I think Lord Leadpipe wants to say something," Jimmy said in a quieter voice.

"Really?" said Grandpa, as though he had no intention of listening.

"I just wanted to say," said Lord Leadpipe, "that I have made special arrangements to help you deal with the . . . uh . . . chilly circumstances in which you find yourself. My Robot Coordinator, Joshua Johnson, will be coming to see you soon. He will have thermal clothing to keep you warm, including my brand-new invention — a pair of Leadpipe Industries' very own HotFoot™ thermal socks. Oh yes, there he is now." Lord Leadpipe pointed to the far end of the workshop.

Jimmy glanced over at Sammy and Maximus. Joshua Johnson had just arrived at Sammy's pit area. The Robot Coordinator looked even stranger than the last time Jimmy had seen him. From the waist up, he looked like his usual self in a dark blazer with the gold L for Leadpipe on the breast pocket and a bright green tie around his neck. From the waist down, he was still wearing brown furry pants and furry boots. With Joshua were three men in brown overalls, unloading towers of cardboard boxes from a huge cart.

"One box of thermal underwear," Joshua was saying, reading from his clipboard. "Fourteen pairs of HotFoot™ thermal socks . . . four pairs of snow boots . . ."

"And that's not all," Lord Leadpipe continued. "My second surprise of the day is that each racer is being assigned a mechanic."

"A mechanic?" blustered Grandpa, his cheeks reddening again. "We have one of those, thank you. Me!"

"Yes, yes, Wilfred, but this is an extra mechanic," explained Lord Leadpipe quietly and patiently, "to help you prepare for the extreme

Arctic racing conditions that your grandson will be facing. And not just any mechanic. Even as we speak, six of the finest pit stop mechanics are leaving Leadpipe Racing Headquarters in a robocopter."

"Really?" cried Jimmy. "Wow! I wonder which one we'll be working with, Grandpa."

His stomach rumbled with excitement. Some of those mechanics were almost as famous as the drivers they worked for: Ryan the Wrench, Easy-Grease McGraw, Pete Webber — they could change a tire in under three seconds with one hand while refueling a pair of turbo rocket-boosters with the other.

"I don't want anyone else meddling with Maverick," Grandpa grumbled. "I don't want some young whippersnapper poking around under his hood with a wrench, breaking things and undoing all my hard work."

"But Grandpa," said Jimmy urgently, "it would be good to have some help. We only have a day to get ready for the race. The Robot Races mechanics know all about racing in the Arctic."

Leadpipe nodded. "Yes. We were up here two years ago," he said, "for the final leg of the championship when Big Al and Crusher had that incident with a polar bear."

"Please, Grandpa," pleaded Jimmy. "With a Robot Races mechanic on the team, we'll be much better prepared for the race!"

There was a long pause. Jimmy held his breath.

"All right, then," Grandpa sighed eventually. "I suppose I could do with a little help. It might be nice to have someone a little younger to carry those heavy snow tires and make the tea. When is he getting here, Leadpipe, this mechanic of yours?"

Leadpipe pulled a gold watch on a chain out from the inside of his fur-lined jacket. "In fifty-eight minutes," he said.

"An hour?" questioned Grandpa. "Tell him to get a move on. We have a race to get ready for!"

CHAPTER 4
MEET PETE

"The question is," said Grandpa, "which route should we take? Over the ice, through the snow, or across the sea?"

Jimmy and Grandpa were looking at a map of the three possible race routes on the Cabcom, Maverick's communication system.

"The ice is fast." Jimmy nodded thoughtfully.

"But slippery," added Grandpa. "One false move and you're skidding into the sea."

"The snow track's much shorter," said Jimmy.

"But it'll be slow with all those snowdrifts," said Grandpa.

"And the crevasses," added Maverick. "If you fall down one of those, you don't come back up in a hurry." He shuddered so hard at the thought of disappearing down a freezing-cold chasm that his windows started to rattle.

"What about the sea track?" he asked. "I bet none of the others will pick that! We would have the place to ourselves. Rolling along through the waves . . ."

"Have you disconnected your huge computer brain?" said Grandpa in astonishment. "You're barely even waterproof!"

"I've got an EFD!" replied Maverick.

"The Emergency Flotation Device?" said Jimmy. "The one Grandpa made out of our old pool floaty?"

"Yup," said Maverick.

"Maverick," said Jimmy with a hint of impatience, "the E stands for Emergency. It means it's for emergency use only. We can't use it all the time."

"It'll be fine!" exclaimed Maverick. "It's tough like me. We could do it, Jimmy!"

"No, we couldn't," said Jimmy. "Even if it did keep us afloat, we wouldn't get anywhere fast on it. We would just be drifting around, bobbing up and down when we could be racing ahead and winning."

Maverick went quiet for a moment. "Let's do the snow then!" he said with renewed excitement.

"I don't know, Maverick. Don't you think we'd be better off on the ice?" said Jimmy.

"I want to do the snow!" shouted Maverick.

"We have to pick the best route," Jimmy said determinedly. "I want Lord Leadpipe's special prize."

Grandpa rolled his eyes. "It's probably an air freshener or a little Leadpipe doll to hang off Maverick's rearview mirror."

"No, Grandpa, it's a really special prize. Lord Leadpipe said so."

"Loonpipe says a lot of things," said Grandpa, "and most of them are nonsense."

"It's probably a brand-new robot racer," Maverick said. He sighed and then continued,

"A top-of-the-range, super-high-tech, shiny, new robot racer." Maverick sighed again. "Don't worry about me, Jimmy. I'll be fine."

"What are you talking about?" exclaimed Jimmy. "I don't care if it's a new rocketship! I'm not racing in any robot except you, Maverick. We're a team and that's that."

"Really?" said Maverick.

"Really," said Jimmy firmly.

Grandpa put an arm around Jimmy's shoulder and squeezed, a proud smile on his face. And Maverick seemed to get a few inches taller as his tires inflated with pride.

Behind them someone cleared his throat.

Jimmy and Grandpa jumped and turned around. A mountain of a man was staring at them. He was easily over six feet tall with a bright red baseball cap on backward. Huge muscles bulged from the short sleeves of his plaid shirt.

"Jimmy Roberts?" said the man.

Jimmy's mouth fell open. "You're — you're — you're — you're —" he stammered.

"Who are you?" asked Grandpa politely.

"He's Pete Webber!" cried Jimmy. "He's Big Al and Crusher's pit stop mechanic! He's the best!"

Pete Webber nodded just once, but said nothing.

"I'm Wilfred Roberts, Jimmy's grandfather and Maverick's inventor," said Grandpa, smiling and shaking Pete's hand.

"Pleased to meet you," growled Pete Webber in a voice so low it sounded like he was at the bottom of a very deep coal mine.

"Have you — are you — will you . . .?" said Jimmy.

"You must be the mechanic Lord Leadpipe said would be coming to work with us," said Grandpa.

Pete nodded again.

"Really?" said Jimmy, his voice so loud and shrill with excitement that it made Maverick jump.

Pete nodded for a third time. "I've been thinking about these Arctic conditions you'll be racing in," he said. "Now, I've seen Jimmy and Maverick race —"

"Really?" Jimmy gasped. "You've seen us? Really?" He tried not to explode with happiness.

Pete bobbed his head again before continuing, "So I think I've got some ideas that will help you two."

"Oh, good," Grandpa said with a smile. "So have I. I've been thinking about additional antifreeze in the coolant, probably some modifications to the vents to maintain engine temperature. I've been toying with the idea of a new spoiler to improve traction as well."

Pete nodded his approval. "Have you thought about redoing the heat exchanger to move more warm air into the cockpit without wasting energy?" he asked.

"Yes, it's a question of making best use of the laws of thermodynamics," said Grandpa, nodding his head in agreement.

"And achieving equivalence in heat distribution to ensure maximum efficiency," Pete added.

Grandpa grinned, his mustache bobbing up and down in agreement. Jimmy looked from Grandpa to Pete in confusion. This technical talk was making his head spin! He still couldn't believe Pete was helping him!

"And in the gadgets department," Grandpa went on, "I was thinking about some kind of hammer or axe to smash through the ice."

"Yeah," growled Pete approvingly. Jimmy thought he saw a glimmer of excitement in the mechanic's dark eyes. "A huge hammer. A massive hammer. Spring-loaded. Hydraulic retraction. Turbocharged."

"Now it's funny you should say that," said Grandpa, beaming. "I'll get us a cup of tea and a chocolate biscuit. When I get back, I'll show you an idea I've been working on . . ."

Pete nodded. "Sounds good."

Jimmy grinned. He had a feeling those two were going to get along pretty well after all. Then he tried to stifle a jaw-breaking yawn. It had been a long day, and he needed to get some sleep before race day.

"Don't worry, Jimmy," said Grandpa. "Our new friend Pete and I can handle it from here if you want to catch up on your sleep. You've got a long day ahead of you tomorrow."

"Okay then. Good night, Grandpa. Good night, Pete. Good night, Maverick," Jimmy said with another yawn.

"Sleep tight," called Maverick as Jimmy began to wander off to his cabin. "Don't let the computer bugs bite."

Two minutes later, Jimmy was wrapped up in bed beneath two duvets and a thick blanket, listening to the howling, freezing wind outside.

Even though this was going to be his third race, he still couldn't quite believe it. Tomorrow he, Jimmy Roberts, would be driving in the Robot Races, across the Arctic Circle, with Pete Webber on his team.

Unbelievable, he thought, as he drifted off to sleep.

★ ★ ★

The next morning, Jimmy woke up still dreaming of the upgrade he might get if he won the Arctic race — sonic-boom rocket-boosters to take Maverick beyond the speed of sound, a robocopter-converter to take Maverick into the air at the flick of a switch . . .

Jimmy sat up and yawned. He couldn't wait to see the modifications Grandpa and Pete had made to Maverick overnight. He threw on his clothes and ran from his cabin to Grandpa's workstation.

He found Grandpa, Maverick, and Pete Webber exactly where he had left them, surrounded by more empty coffee mugs and plates than he could count.

"Morning, Jimmy," yawned Grandpa.

"Hey, Jimmy," said Pete.

"What a night!" called Maverick. "Wait 'til you see what we've been up to!"

"Show me!" said Jimmy, putting his head in Maverick's window and examining the control panel. "Hey, Grandpa, what does the orange lever do?"

Grandpa said nothing.

"Grandpa?"

Jimmy turned. Grandpa seemed to have gone to sleep facedown in his mug.

"Your grandpa's had a long night," whispered Pete. "He's some genius, I tell you. It's no wonder you're doing so well in the race."

"And now we're going to do even better with you on the team," whispered Jimmy. "That special upgrade prize is going to be mine for sure!"0

"Hey, Wilf," Pete whispered in Grandpa's ear. "Wake up and show your boy what Maverick's got up his sleeves."

Grandpa's head jerked up. "What's that?" he mumbled. "Yes, what was I saying?"

"You were just telling me about the modifications you and Pete have been working on," Jimmy said, smiling.

"Ah, yes," said Grandpa, stroking his mustache back into position and clearing his throat. "Yes, well . . . see the orange lever? Pull it and see what happens."

Jimmy tugged on the orange lever. A rhythmic thumping boomed out, making the whole airship shake. Maverick jumped up and down in time with the pounding beat, and the pit area echoed with the sound of ripping metal. Jimmy looked around in horror and realized Grandpa was shouting something at him.

"Turn it off!" bellowed Grandpa.

Jimmy pushed the orange lever back, and the thumping stopped as suddenly as it had started.

"Wow!" cried Maverick. "What a mover!"

"Oops," said Grandpa with a grin. "I didn't expect it to make quite that much of a racket."

"That's your robo-pummeler," said Pete Webber. "A massive, turbo-sprung jackhammer bolted to Maverick's underside. It can squash snow to make the ground smoother, so you'll be able to turn a snowdrift into an ice road in about three seconds."

"And knock a hole in the floor of an airship in about two seconds," said Grandpa, looking nervously around to see if anyone had noticed the damage they had done.

"And then there's the roto-blade," explained Pete. "You push that green button next to the orange lever, and a razor-sharp circular saw with huge teeth extends from Maverick's roof. It's telescopic, can pivot in any direction, and will cut through anything — ice, compacted snow, rock — you name it."

"Wow," said Jimmy, leaning in and pressing the button.

Bang!

A huge parachute was fired from Maverick's roof. It slowly floated down and covered all of them.

"Oops," said Jimmy. "I thought you said it was the green button!"

"Shall I repackage?" came Maverick's voice through the darkness beneath the parachute.

"Good idea," said Grandpa.

"You need to be careful," said Pete when Maverick had retracted the parachute and folded it back into his roof. "The dark green button releases the parachute. The light green button activates the roto-blade."

Jimmy peered at the buttons. "You could have chosen another color," he muttered.

"There are some other things you should know," continued Pete. "I've put my spare toolkit in the trunk. Remember that there are no pit stops in this race. You may need to do some repairs while you're out on the ice. I can talk you through anything you're not sure about over the Cabcom."

"And we've put snow tires on, of course," added Grandpa, "but if it gets really slippery out there you can activate a set of snow chains with that blue button," he said, pointing to it on Maverick's dashboard. "Press it and they will automatically wrap around Maverick's tires. You will probably lose a little speed, but what you lose in pace you'll gain in grip."

"That's about it," said Pete. But Jimmy didn't hear him. The mechanic's voice was drowned out by the sound of a warning siren booming around the pit area, the creaking groan of the airship's huge steel door being opened, and a biting blast of cold air whistling past their ears.

"Drivers, you have just five minutes until the race begins," echoed the voice of Lord Leadpipe. "That's five minutes until the race begins," he repeated.

Jimmy took a deep breath and smiled at Grandpa and Pete. "This is it," he said, climbing into Maverick's cockpit.

"Good luck, my boy," said Grandpa, winking and grinning proudly.

Pete gave a nod. "See you at the finish line," he growled, but there was a warm smile on his face.

Jimmy fired up Maverick's engines and looked out through his windshield, through the airship door to the Arctic ice. Blinding white, it gleamed in the sunlight, stretching to a brilliant blue sky. It looked like the edge of the world.

Jimmy guided Maverick down the ramp onto the ice.

Race marshals with flags lined the route to the start line. They waved him forward and into his starting position. The start line was right next to Lord Leadpipe's igloo. There were no grandstands for this leg of the championship, as it was far too cold and dangerous for crowds to gather. But it seemed as if every camerabot in the world had made it instead. The hovering robotic cameras sprayed deicer onto their lenses to stop their cameras from instantly freezing over.

Jimmy knew that there would be millions of people sitting in their living rooms at home, edging closer to the screen and feeling the excitement that only the Robot Races could cause. The idea of all those people watching him made his stomach do a somersault.

Instead of the usual cheering from the crowds, all Jimmy could hear was the howling of the wind. It whipped around the robots and stirred up a blizzard in front of the racers' eyes.

The racers pulled up to the start line: Monster and Missy, Kako and Lightning, Chip and Dug, Sammy and Maximus, and lastly, Horace and Zoom. Each one of the robots looked like they had been freshly painted and polished, with shiny new stickers advertising their sponsors. Even Maverick had a new That's Shallot! sticker on his hood. The stupid onion logo was just the same though. At least it was better than nothing.

The camerabots darted among them, and huge images of each racer appeared on the airship's massive display screens. None of the drivers looked at each other. They were all staring anxiously down the track at what lay ahead.

Lord Leadpipe's track engineers had been busy overnight. They had cut a massive channel in a straight line through the snow and built its banks up, so the track curved up at the edges like a bobsled run. It was a half-pipe, a giant U-shape in the distance, reaching all the way to the horizon.

"Racers," Lord Leadpipe's voice boomed from the loudspeakers, "the first ten-mile stretch of the race will be a straight sprint down the track, which I'm calling the Arctic Roll! At the end of the Roll, you'll come to a crossroads. It's left for the snow route, straight ahead for the ice route, and right for the sea route. The race will begin in ten . . . nine . . ."

"Which route are we taking, Jimmy?" asked Maverick, revving his engines and running some last minute software checks.

Jimmy felt a cold lump spread down his throat like he'd just swallowed a lump of ice. He, Grandpa, and Pete had spent so long talking about Maverick's improvements that they had forgotten to choose which route to take!

"Four . . . three . . ." echoed the countdown.

"We need to decide, Jimmy," said Maverick, "because we're off!"

CHAPTER 5
INTO THE UNKNOWN

"Two . . . one . . . GO! GO! GO!" cried
Lord Leadpipe standing on the top of his igloo,
microphone in hand. His voice was almost
drowned out by the roar of engines and the
howl of the Arctic wind.

All six racers shot away from the start line,
skidding and sliding, bouncing over the snow
like bumper cars. The ground beneath them
screamed as the racers' spinning tires sprayed
chips of ice and sent columns of steam and
smoke into the air.

Jimmy gripped the steering wheel, his
knuckles turning white. He pulled ahead of

Princess Kako, who was struggling to keep her robobike, Lightning, upright while dodging the other racers as they spun and skidded toward her. Sammy and Horace also seemed to be having slow starts, but Missy looked less worried about bumps — she was laughing as the other racers jumped and swerved. Missy put her foot down on the accelerator and Monster's enormous bulk tore off into the lead.

"What a mess!" said Jimmy, glancing at the chaos in his rearview mirror as the flying snow made it difficult to see who was where.

"Never mind them," said Maverick. "Let's try to stay up front and out of trouble."

Chip and Dug were in hot pursuit of Missy, so Jimmy tucked Maverick in behind them, using Dug as a buffer against the wind.

"Great start, Jimmy," said Maverick.

"Time to get in the lead," said Jimmy, gritting his teeth and turning the steering wheel to pull out from behind Chip and Dug and overtake them. Maverick swerved wildly and started skidding to the side at a terrifying speed.

"What's wrong with the steering, Maverick?" cried Jimmy anxiously. "What's going on?"

"Aquaplaning!" said Maverick. "Dug's exhaust is melting the snow. We're surfing on top of the snow at the moment!"

The steering wheel continued to jerk left and right, and Jimmy felt like he was juggling a bar of soap as it slipped through his fingers.

"Should we activate the snow chains?" asked Maverick as they moved from side to side.

"Not right now. We just need to get away from Dug's exhaust," decided Jimmy. He took his foot off the accelerator and let Maverick drop back. With one sharp twitch on the steering wheel, Jimmy managed to guide Maverick out to the right and onto solid snow. Jimmy stomped on the accelerator.

"I've stabilized wheelspin," said Maverick, his revs rising as they rocketed forward. "Now we're motoring!" he cried as they pushed past Dug into second place.

Looking in his rearview mirror, Jimmy could see Chip's racer lagging farther behind. While the track was like this, the diggerbot's caterpillar tracks weren't as effective as Maverick's tires.

"The path is getting narrower," said Jimmy after a few minutes. "Soon there won't be room for passing. We need to get around Missy before it's too late —"

Before he could finish, Jimmy saw a flash in his rearview mirror as Sammy and Maximus shot past Chip. "Looks like Sammy's making the most of his new fan blades. He'll be past us in a second," Jimmy murmured.

"Look how fast Maximus is on this snow," Maverick said as the hoverbot swept past them and settled smoothly into second place.

Jimmy looked down at his GPS display on the Cabcom and saw that all six racers were now close together as the snowy road narrowed. This was going to be quite the race!

"Maverick, can you find the best route through?" cried Jimmy.

"I'm trying!" said Maverick.

Just at that moment, Jimmy felt a bump as Maverick hit a pothole in the icy surface of the half-pipe. The jolt made the wheel lock up, and Maverick was sent skidding at a 45-degree angle to the track.

"Whoa!" said Maverick as slushy snow sprayed out in every direction.

As Maverick skidded, Jimmy jabbed at the blue button on his dashboard. There was a metallic clunk and a clacking noise as specially-made chains snaked around the tires.

"Snow chains engaged," said Maverick. "We've got control back. Great idea, Jimmy."

"Thanks, Maverick," Jimmy said with a grin. He eased Maverick back into a straight line and squeezed the accelerator once more.

They had lost a few valuable seconds, and now Chip and Dug were right on their tails again.

Trapped between Dug and Maximus, Jimmy tried to hold Maverick steady. As they were squeezed tighter and tighter between the two massive robots, the back of Maximus's inflatable air cushions skimmed Maverick's front bumper.

"What are they doing?" asked Jimmy.

"Trying to knock us out of the way, I think," said Maverick cheerily.

"Sammy wouldn't do that!" cried Jimmy, desperately hoping he was right.

Sure enough, Sammy's face popped up on the Cabcom screen. "Sorry, Jimmy!" he yelled. "This snow is slippery, isn't it?"

Maximus veered toward them again, hitting Maverick a glancing blow that sent him flying sideways and up the side of the Arctic Roll.

"Strap on your circuit boards!" cried Maverick as they veered back into the path of Chip and Dug.

With a deafening crack and a blinding flash, Dug suddenly glowed blue.

Jimmy gritted his teeth as Maverick hit Dug's blue light and was flung away.

"What's that?" asked Jimmy.

"An electro-force field," said Maverick as they sailed toward Maximus.

"I feel like a pinball!" shrieked Maverick as they bounced between the two towering racers on either side of them.

"And it looks like the track's just about to narrow even more when we get to that bend," Jimmy said, looking at the steep sides to the course. "There's only one thing for it." He stomped on the accelerator again and yanked on the steering wheel. Veering sharply to the left, Maverick rocketed up the bank of the Arctic Roll half-pipe.

"What are you doing?" cried Maverick. "I'm the wrong way up!"

"Hold on," Jimmy said calmly. "We're going to keep out of trouble and take the high side of the curve. Then we'll slingshot right past the others. Keep your pistons pumping and we'll be fine."

"Gotcha, Jimmy. Full power coming right up."

Maverick adjusted his settings, and the engine roared with more power. Jimmy was thrown back in his seat as they skimmed the very top of the half-pipe. He could feel the G-force squeezing his face and trying to pry his hands off the steering wheel as they hurtled through the bend. For one terrifying moment, he thought that the tires were losing grip and they might topple sideways and roll back down the hill to get crushed under Dug's wheels. But the snow chains bit deep into the high sides of the bend, and they held firm. Then Jimmy gave a little twist of the steering wheel and Maverick arced downward. Using the slope to pick up extra speed, they shot downhill and flew ahead of both Sammy and Chip.

They were back in second place behind Missy and Monster.

Maverick let out a loud yell as they hit the bottom of the slope again. "Amaaaaaaaaaaazing!" he shouted. "Nice thinking, Jimmy . . . and excellent work by me, obviously."

Grandpa's face popped up on the Cabcom. He must have had his face pressed right up to the camera, because all Jimmy could see was a huge grin and an even bigger mustache.

"That was incredible. Quick thinking, Jimmy boy. Well done!"

"Thanks, Grandpa," said Jimmy.

"And Pete's had a message from Big Al," Grandpa went on. "He says . . . what did he say, Pete?"

Jimmy heard Pete mumbling something in the background.

"Big Al says he could learn a thing or two from you!"

"What?" cried Jimmy. He was so amazed that he veered slightly off course.

"And I bet I could teach that Crusher a thing or two as well," Maverick boasted.

"Anyway," Grandpa went on, "you have about two miles until the track splits. Do you know what route you're going to take?"

"The snow track, I think," replied Jimmy. "At least I'll be able to keep an eye on the others."

"You're the boss," said Maverick. "I'm just as happy crashing through the ice into the sea as I am dropping down a crevasse and never being seen again. I think they're both great ideas."

"Thanks," said Jimmy flatly. "That's really helpful."

"One mile until the track splits," came Grandpa's voice again. "It's about to get interesting, my boy!"

★ ★ ★

As they approached the last few hundred feet of the Arctic Roll, the gaps between the racers tightened once more. They were jammed together nose to tail as they powered through the half-pipe.

"Breathe in, Maverick! We're getting squeezed," said Jimmy as the steep walls came dangerously close to taking off Maverick's side mirrors.

Behind them, Dug and Maximus were both sending up a flurry of snow as they sped along.

"Hey!" cried Chip over the Cabcom. "This track is ruining my bodywork!"

Up in front, Maverick could see Monster's huge body scraping the frozen walls as well. Jimmy could hear Missy over the radio, shouting encouragement at her racer. "Come on, you lazy lump of dingo dung! It's just some frozen water. Power on through!"

"Good point," said Maverick. "I like her style."

"We've made it to the crossroads. Here we go!" shouted Jimmy as all six racers hurtled out of the half-pipe and onto the open section of the course.

In the distance, Jimmy could see snow-covered peaks to the left, a gray sea speckled with ice floes to the right, and, at its edges, ice cliffs like sharp, jagged teeth. Straight ahead, a narrow ice track stretched to the horizon.

"Still want the snow track, Jimmy?" asked Maverick. "The snow on those mountains looks pretty deep."

"And those clouds look like they're just about ready to dump a whole lot more snow," Jimmy agreed.

He paused for a second . . . then came to a decision.

"Hold on to your hat, Maverick. We're taking the ice!"

CHAPTER 6
DANCING ON ICE

"Did you hear that, Grandpa?" Jimmy said, punching a button on the Cabcom.

"I can hear you, my boy. You do whatever your gut says is right," said Grandpa.

"Thanks, Grandpa. Anyway, the ice can't be that thin, can it?"

"Do you have your scarf on?" asked Grandpa.

"Yes," Jimmy said. He sighed. "And my thermal vest."

"Good," said Grandpa. "Now when you get onto the ice, keep it steady. If you go too fast, you'll lose control. And you need to keep an eye out for —"

"Hold on a sec, Grandpa," Jimmy interrupted as he spotted something ahead. "What's that?" He punched a button on the dashboard, and one section of the windshield zoomed in on the route as if he was peering through binoculars. As the track opened up onto an expanse of ice, the wind picked up and w hipped dangerously at each of the racers.

"Markers up ahead," said Maverick, detecting them on his screen. "Left for the snow route, straight ahead for the ice route, and right for the sea route."

Sure enough, there lay the faint outlines of a track, and off to the left side there was a sign, which read: "BEWARE: Racers failing to stay within the track markings risk straying onto thin ice. Any robot requiring the assistance of Leadpipe safetybots will be disqualified from the race."

"If we get into trouble, we'll be rescued," Jimmy said grimly, "but we'll be out of the race!" He squinted into the distance. Snow was beginning to fall now, but he could see sweeping lines across the ice like the impressions left by ice skaters on a rink — except much wider and deeper. *Those must be the track markings,* he thought.

"Hold onto your hats," Jimmy yelled. "Can you get a reading on the ice route, Maverick? Will it take our weight?"

"Computing," replied Maverick with a whir of his hard drive. "Looks good," he concluded. "The route marked out is easily thick enough, with no dangerous cracks detected. We should be fine."

Jimmy hunched lower over the wheel and peered through the whizzing windshield wipers at the ice track ahead.

Suddenly Lightning surged up through the pack, using first Dug, then Maximus, then Monster to shelter from the wind. Then the robobike streaked ahead of them all before swinging out to the right and making for the dangers of the Arctic Ocean.

Behind Maverick, Horace and Zoom were neck and neck with Sammy and Maximus.

Horace swung left, straight into Maximus, trying to barge the hoverbot out of the way. Instead, his sleek black robot, shaped like a sports car, slapped straight into Maximus's air cushions and was sent spinning away. By the time Horace had regained control, he was a long way back.

"Ha," said Jimmy triumphantly. "Serves him right."

Jimmy looked into his rearview mirror and caught a flash of yellow and gold as Chip sent Dug roaring off to the left and up toward the snow-covered peaks. Just ahead of them were Missy and Monster.

"Just as I thought, Maverick. Those two racers are the best equipped to deal with the tough snow terrain."

"And it looks like they are making quick work of things already!" replied Maverick as Dug and Monster quickly climbed through the deep snowdrifts, scattering an avalanche of white powder behind them.

"Wow, look at Princess Kako go," Jimmy said, turning his attention to the right side of the crossroads where Lightning was sprinting toward the ocean. "I hope she knows what she's doing."

With a final burst of acceleration, Lightning rocketed off the edge, diving through the air toward the sea track, which was marked by bobbing Leadpipe buoys. As he flew, Lightning's wheels folded in, and a propeller emerged from somewhere beneath his robobike body. By the time he hit the water, Lightning had transformed into a jet ski with Kako perched comfortably on top. The girl in silver simply hunched lower over her racer and skimmed out to sea in a storm of spray. She zipped between the floating rocks of ice, getting farther and farther into the distance until she disappeared from sight.

Jimmy knew that the viewers watching at home would love that maneuver. He hoped one of the camerabots had caught it.

Sammy and Maximus followed Kako and Lightning onto the water, his hoverbot air cushions gliding smoothly off the edge of the ice and onto the water without a bump. His huge turbo-propellers left a mist of sea spray behind them.

"Come on, Jimmy. It's time to show these piles of junk what we've got," Maverick said, and Jimmy turned his attention back to the ice ahead.

"Get ready, Maverick. Things are about to get slippery," Jimmy warned. And with that, they raced through an opening between the ice cliffs and onto the ice track.

"Woo-hoo!" cried Maverick.

"Remember, Maverick," said Jimmy. "Dug and Monster have gone up onto the snow track. It's a much shorter route."

"We'll be faster," said Maverick confidently, adjusting his balance. "You watch me. Lightning and Maximus might be fast on the water too, but they're no match for us on this ice."

"And it's just us on the ice track," added Jimmy.

"Even better," said Maverick with satisfaction. "No one to put us off our game."

"No competition," said Jimmy with a smile. "We're going to —"

Jimmy stopped talking and listened. There was a low rumble coming from somewhere behind them. It was getting louder. Jimmy glanced in his rearview mirror. Through the falling snow, he could just make out a black shape coming up behind them. As it drew nearer, the sound got louder and clearer.

"Oh, no," Jimmy said, groaning.

"Horace Pelly and Zoom are right behind us," announced Maverick. "And they're coming up fast."

CHAPTER 7
OFF ICE

"Zoom's gaining on us," said Maverick grimly.

"What can we do?" asked Jimmy as he steered into a wide bend in the ice track.

"My sensors tell me I'm at top speed on this ice," said Maverick. "I'm just about hanging onto it. If we go any faster, I'm not sure I can stay in control. Anything could happen," he warned, "but we could fire the rocket-boosters."

"No," replied Jimmy firmly. "This ice is too fragile for that. We would burn a hole straight through to the ocean. We're going to have to come up with something else."

There was a moment's silence while Jimmy sat and thought. He looked in Maverick's rearview mirror again. Zoom filled it. He was right behind them, and Jimmy could see the outline of Horace hunched over his steering wheel, his perfect white teeth gritted in concentration. Suddenly Zoom swung away, out of sight.

"They're pulling out to the right," said Maverick. "They're going for an overtake."

"Are you sure we can't go any faster?" asked Jimmy.

"Not if you want to keep going in a straight line and stay alive," said Maverick.

"That gives me an idea!" said Jimmy. He jerked the steering wheel to the right. Maverick veered in front of Zoom, blocking the move.

"Recalculating traction!" screamed Maverick as they slid across the ice, all four of his wheels spinning and sliding sideways.

"Straight line!" Jimmy grinned. "Good idea, Maverick. If they can't get past us, they can't get ahead!"

Horace didn't dare drive off the track onto the thinner part of the ice sheet. Zoom pulled back to the left and began to accelerate.

"They're going for it again," said Maverick.

Jimmy jerked the wheel back to the left. Maverick hurtled back toward the center of the ice track, blocking Zoom again.

"That scared them away!" said Maverick triumphantly. "They're backing off!"

Jimmy snatched another look in Maverick's rearview mirror. Maverick was right. Zoom had dropped right back.

Cabcom crackled into life. There was Horace Pelly's face filling the screen. "Having trouble steering that old bucket of yours?" sneered Horace.

"Having trouble overtaking us in that tin can of yours?" replied Jimmy.

"Oh, I'll win this race, Jimmy," said Horace. "Don't you worry about that. That super-awesome Leadpipe upgrade will be mine. Not that I need it, of course. Whatever the upgrade is, I'll probably have one already — so it'll probably be a downgrade for me. But I'd still like to win it — just to stop you from having it."

Jimmy rolled his eyes and sighed. "Have you almost finished talking?" he asked.

"Just one last thing," said Horace, grinning slyly. "Remember this face." He pushed his nose into the screen. "Take a good look. This is the face you'll see at the top of the winners' podium."

"Don't look at his face, Jimmy. It'll make you feel sick," Maverick said, laughing.

"How hilarious," said Horace flatly. "We'll see who's laughing at the finish line, shall we, Maverick?"

Cabcom went blank.

"He can't get past us," said Jimmy, nodding confidently. "The track's too narrow here."

"But look ahead," replied Maverick. "It's opening up again in just a few hundred feet! This section of ice must be much stronger."

Zoom soon appeared on Maverick's right-hand side again. Jimmy glanced over to see Horace Pelly grinning through his window at him and waving. Then Horace reached down and pressed a button on the dashboard.

"Oh, no!" said Jimmy. "I hope he hasn't just —"

With a rush of flame and a huge boom, Horace's rocket-boosters fired. He shot past Jimmy and Maverick and into the lead, melting the ice as he went.

"We're losing grip, Jimmy," said Maverick as they skidded left, then right. "Those rockets are turning the ice to water! We're sloshing around with no control at all — our snow chains can't get a hold of the ice."

"I knew using boosters was dangerous," muttered Jimmy. "I'm going to slow down a little, Maverick. We need to go carefully until we get past him."

Just at that moment, Cabcom crackled back into life.

"Not you again!" sighed Jimmy.

"Don't be so rude, Jimmy," said Grandpa.

"Oh, sorry, Grandpa," said Jimmy. "I thought you were Horace."

"Been bothering you, has he?" Grandpa grunted. "You need to get back up there and show him, Jimmy boy. Fire the rocket-boosters and you'll storm ahead!"

"No," said Jimmy, "we can't do that. Horace's boosters have just melted the ice. If we fire Maverick's rocket-boosters too, we could end up breaking the ice and falling into the sea! We're going to have to come up with something else."

"Okay, my boy. It's your call," said Grandpa. "I know you'll think of something."

Cabcom crackled, and the screen went blank again. Jimmy peered ahead at Zoom disappearing into the distance. From underneath Zoom's black body came a strange orange glow. It wasn't his rocket-boosters — they had done their job and burned out long ago.

"Maverick, what's going on ahead?" asked Jimmy urgently as Maverick fought for grip. The steering wheel was jolting wildly in Jimmy's hands. Maverick didn't answer.

"Activate zoom screen," said Jimmy, his voice starting to shake as they swerved.

The zoom screen popped up above the dashboard. It showed Zoom racing ahead, roaring along on a cushion of flame.

"He's using his flamethrowers. And he's pointing them down at the ice!" cried Jimmy. "No wonder we're sliding all over the place."

"It's worse than that," said Maverick urgently. "My sensors warn me that the ice is barely taking our weight. He's not just melting the ice — he's burning through it!"

As Maverick spoke, enormous creaking and groaning sounds ripped through the air, making Jimmy's ears ring and his heart stop. A thin black crack opened up in the ice ahead of them. The crack widened. And then another one opened up. And another.

"The ice is breaking up!" cried Jimmy. "We're going to —"

SPLASH!

Maverick and Jimmy were tipped into the freezing Arctic Ocean!

CHAPTER 8
THAT SINKING FEELING

Jimmy was thrown forward onto the steering wheel as the world disappeared and the gray ocean rose up and swallowed Maverick. They dropped like a stone straight down toward the seabed.

"What do we do? What do we do?" gasped Jimmy.

The faint light through the ice above them was disappearing fast as they plummeted backward into blackness. Through the gloom, Jimmy could just make out three blinking lights that had suddenly appeared on the surface.

Safetybots, he groaned silently.

"Maverick!" he cried as the engine cut out. "Do something! If we don't get back to the surface fast, we'll be fished out and disqualified." Already the temperature in Maverick's cockpit was dropping rapidly as the heaters clogged up with water.

"Oh, no. This doesn't look good at all," wailed Maverick.

"We need to d-d-d-do something. But w-w-w-what?" Even in his HotFoot™ socks and thermal underwear, Jimmy was starting to shiver violently.

The dim light was fading as they sank farther into the blackness of the deep ocean. Dark moving shapes loomed through Maverick's windows. Jimmy couldn't stop himself from wondering whether they could be killer whales or giant squid.

"I can't see a thing," said Jimmy. "Do we have emergency lighting? I need to see the dashboard controls."

"My circuits are f-f-freezing up," stammered Maverick, his voice rising and falling randomly.

"And I'm losing my contact light engine in the boo-boo-boo-booster."

"What?" said Jimmy. "What are you talking about?"

"I d-d-d-d-don't know," stuttered Maverick. "My communication processor thermostat thingy is not responding."

"Gotta think. Gotta think," said Jimmy. He felt like his brain was starting to go numb, like when he ate ice cream too quickly . . .

"Processing unstable," said Maverick, still talking nonsense. "Shut down. Shut down."

Jimmy flicked on the Cabcom. "Grandpa?" he called. "Grandpa, come in." He stared into the blank screen. It was dead.

"There must be something we can use to get us back up to the surface," said Jimmy, thinking aloud. "What do we have?" he went on, thinking through all the gadgets that could save them. "Parachute? No. We want to go up, not down. Roll cage? No. We're not turning over, we're sinking. EFD? Emergency Flotation Device! That's it!" he shrieked. "We need to float. And this is an emergency for certain. Maverick, activate the EFD!"

"Act-act-act —" stammered Maverick.

Nothing happened. Now Jimmy really was on his own. Maverick's central processor was all over the place, and there was no one else to help him. But which button was it? If he got it wrong and released the parachute it would drag them right to the bottom of the sea, far from the reach of any safetybots.

Jimmy gulped. His finger hovered between the many buttons lit up in front of him: red, green, orange, yellow, blue —

Think, Jimmy, think, he said to himself as red lasers pierced the darkness all around him. The safetybots were scanning, preparing to make an extraction. The parachute button was light green . . . no, no — it was dark green. And the roto-blade was light green. The pummeler was that orange lever . . . but what color was the EFD? Jimmy thought back to the last time he had used it, to skim over the quicksand in the jungle. But he had just yelled at Maverick to inflate it. Jimmy shook his head. He had to do something! He thumped the nearest button and prayed he hadn't made a huge mistake.

Hssssssss!

With a rush of air, the dinghy popped out around Maverick's sides. Maverick began to rise through the water in a whirlwind of bubbles. Faster and faster they shot through the water. Jimmy's stomach climbed into his throat and his ears popped like corks as they rocketed to the surface and burst back out into the world in an explosion of water.

When the chaos had calmed, Jimmy peered out of the windshield. They were bobbing on the surface of the sea like they were floating on an inflatable raft. Above his head, the safetybots hummed like angry bees, three large orbs the size of cannonballs spinning in the air. Then after a moment the red flashing lights on the robots blinked green and with a *whirrrrrr*, they zoomed away.

"Are you all right, Maverick?" asked Jimmy once his head had stopped spinning.

"I think so," croaked Maverick. "But I'm not getting any warmer floating around like this. I think it's time to stop swimming and get out!"

"Good plan," said Jimmy, smiling with relief. "But how? Can we pull ourselves out with the grappling hook?"

Jimmy looked around. They were bobbing around at least sixty feet from what looked like a shelf of solid ice.

"I'll give it a try," said Maverick. "The steel cable's ninety feet long. It'll reach the ice, but I don't know if it will hold on. It could crack the ice." And with that, the compartment on his hood slid open and the grappling hooks rose, ready to launch. "Identifying target," said Maverick, his computer scanning the ice shelf for a spot that would take their weight. With a beep, Maverick zeroed in on the best option.

"Fire!"

The hooks flew through the air and sank into the ice with a dull thud.

"It sounds pretty solid," said Jimmy. "Reel it in, Maverick."

"Slowly . . ." said Maverick, reeling in the steel cable. "Slowly . . ."

The cable went taut, and for a second Jimmy thought it had done its job. But then the grappling hook tore away from the ice sheet. It came hurtling back toward them with a rattle and a clank as it skipped over the hard surface.

"It's not holding!" cried Jimmy.

Then the hook suddenly caught again — and this time it bit deep and held firm. Maverick tested his weight on it with a sharp tug.

"It's good!" he cried. "Let's go."

Maverick began to reel in the steel cable, pulling them through the water toward the ice. Jimmy's teeth were gritted, and he was grinding them every inch of the way. In less than a minute, the cable had pulled them through the freezing water to the edge of the ice shelf.

"Go slowly, Maverick," said Jimmy. "We don't want to go through the ice again and end up back where we started."

Inch by inch, the steel cable pulled Maverick's front bumper onto the ice, then his front wheels, then his back wheels. Beneath the robot's tires, there came a creaking and a groaning noise. But the ice stayed in one piece.

Finally they were perched on the ice, seawater pouring out of Maverick.

Jimmy sat for a moment, listening to the sounds of the ice beneath them. Maverick, meanwhile, retracted the EFD and tucked it back into its storage compartment.

"Let's get going!" yelled Maverick. "Don't forget, we have a race to win!"

"You're definitely feeling better," Jimmy said, laughing.

"I'm like a rubber ball," said Maverick. "I bounce back from anything!" He revved his engines, coughing and spluttering the seawater out of his pipes. "Ready?" he said.

"Ready," said Jimmy. He flicked Maverick into first gear and crushed the accelerator pedal with his foot. They were off, roaring back to the ice track and getting back in the race.

"Run a check on all your functions, Maverick," said Jimmy as they sailed over the ice, rising to top speed. Jimmy couldn't believe they were back in the race!

"I'm already on it," said Maverick. "I'm fully rebooted and starting self-repair now. But we better not end up in the water again," he added. "The air canister for the EFD's empty, so we can't use it anymore."

"Horace could have done us some real damage back there," said Jimmy angrily.

"I told you, Jimmy, I'm fine," said Maverick cheerily.

"But after all the hard work Grandpa and Pete put into you, Horace has to go and pull a stunt like that," Jimmy said. He sighed, shook his head, and then continued, "He doesn't care what happens to anyone else as long as he's okay. What an idiot!"

"Speaking of your grandpa, let's tell him we're okay," Maverick suggested.

"Good idea!" Jimmy agreed. "Fire up Cabcom."

"Oh," said Maverick anxiously.

"What's up?" asked Jimmy.

"No problem," said Maverick. "Cabcom's frozen solid, so we're out of contact with the team."

"Can you defrost it?" asked Jimmy.

"I'm trying my best, but it might take a while," said Maverick.

"Okay," said Jimmy. "Time to get even with Horace."

"Get even?" repeated Maverick in surprise.

"Level, I mean," said Jimmy quickly. *And then get even!* he thought. *I'm going to teach Horace Pelly a lesson he will never forget!*

CHAPTER 9
ICEBREAKER

"How are you doing, Maverick?" asked Jimmy a little while later. "Have you warmed up?"

"Heading for optimum temperature and speed," said Maverick. "Getting warmer . . . even warmer . . . we're red-hot and racing!"

Maverick's tires ate up the ground. His engines roaring loud and clear once again. The ice stretched in every direction, flat and smooth and white and empty.

"We must be miles behind Horace," Jimmy said, sighing. "And without Cabcom we have no idea how far ahead he is."

"Oh!" said Maverick. "I've got a surprise."

A panel slid back on Maverick's dashboard. A circle of green glass appeared. It lit up, and a line of green light swept around the circle like the minute hand on a watch. Every time the line swept over a little green blob, the machine made a *ping!* sound.

"What is it?" asked Jimmy.

"Pete installed it last night," explained Maverick. "It's called a radar. They used it in the olden days. Grandpa knows all about them, anyway."

"Why do we have it? What does it do?" asked Jimmy.

"See that little green blob?" said Maverick. "That's Horace."

"Really?" exclaimed Jimmy. "It's pretty good for an antique, isn't it?"

"Pete said Crusher's communications system is always going down. Big Al uses radar all the time. He says it's basic but more reliable. With this we'll be able to locate any robot within a ten-mile radius."

"So how far ahead is Horace?"

"Two miles," said Maverick. "But we're gaining on him."

Jimmy peered at the radar. The little green blob was getting closer, but Jimmy couldn't see any sign of Horace and Zoom.

A thin coating of snow landed on the windshield.

"Weather warning," announced Maverick. "There's a snowstorm coming in from the north."

Already, the flakes of snow had thickened. They flew at Maverick's windshield as he raced into the storm, splatting on the glass in big white blotches.

"Activate screen clearance," said Jimmy.

Maverick set his windshield wipers to the fastest speed and the hot air was blasting inside, but the snow was flying thicker and faster than he could clear it. It began to creep up the windshield. Jimmy hunched over the steering wheel. All he could see was a solid white curtain of flakes flying at him.

"We're going to have to slow down, Maverick," said Jimmy. "This is dangerous." He eased his foot off the accelerator, and little by little, the green blob on the radar moved farther and farther away from them.

"Horace and Zoom are getting away!" said Maverick anxiously. "We'll never catch them if we crawl along like this."

"We'll never catch them if we drop off the ice or fall down a hole because we can't see where we're going!" said Jimmy.

"There must be something we can do," grumbled Maverick.

"Hold on," said Jimmy. "I've got it!"

"What are you going to do?"

"You know your engine cooling system?" asked Jimmy.

"Yes," said Maverick.

"It sucks in cold air, doesn't it?" Jimmy asked excitedly.

"That's right," said Maverick.

"Maverick, can you reverse it and spray out hot air instead?"

"Consider it done," said Maverick.

Just like when he was using the grappling hook, the compartment in Maverick's hood slid open. But it wasn't the grappling hook launcher that rose. It was a huge pipe, like a vacuum cleaner, pointing out into the wall of flying snow.

"Activating snow clearance," announced Maverick with ice-cool calm.

All of a sudden, a large, round hole appeared in the snowstorm: a tunnel through the blizzard of snowflakes. The snowstorm raged around them, but for at least fifteen feet in front of the car it was crystal clear.

"It works!" cried Maverick in amazement.

"Great," said Jimmy.

"Genius!" said Maverick. "Now let's get moving. We have a race to win!"

Jimmy slammed his foot on the accelerator again and pinned his eyes to the tunnel through the snowstorm.

"I can just about see where we're going," he said, "but I can't see if we're going the right way.

You might have to navigate for me so I don't steer us back into the sea."

"Our GPS stopped working in the storm," Maverick replied. "We could end up racing back to the start line if we're not careful."

"What about the radar?" asked Jimmy.

"It can help us track Horace," Maverick said, "but it can't show us the route."

"Well, let's follow Horace!" Jimmy said, grinning. "He can actually help us for once!"

"Got it," Maverick replied, revving his engine.

It took a while, but soon they were out of the storm. Up ahead of them, Jimmy could just make out a distant black blur.

"It's Horace and Zoom," he said, "and they're swerving all over the place!"

"Looks like that snow has caused them a few technical problems," Maverick said, laughing.

"We're going to catch up to them," said Jimmy as they raced toward Horace, who was still veering from one side of the track to the other.

Jimmy came roaring up behind them. As he and Maverick got closer they could see Horace thumping Zoom's steering wheel, shouting, and flicking switches on and off furiously.

But just as they were about to pull up next to them and overtake, a huge cloud of snow exploded like an enormous sneeze from somewhere underneath Zoom.

Vrmmm! Vrmmm! Zoom's engine let out a deep, powerful growl, and then he took off again.

"He's gotten the snow out of his system," said Maverick, "and he's back on track."

"And we're back in the race," said Jimmy. "But I wish we could get him back for melting the ice and putting us in danger," he added angrily.

Jimmy was sick of seeing Horace Pelly playing dirty tricks in the Robot Races championship. For once he wanted to give Horace a taste of his own medicine.

"That's it!" he cried. "The robo-pummeler. If we can just get ahead by a hundred, maybe a hundred and fifty feet, we can use it to crack a huge hole in the ice. Horace will be falling down it before he even knows it's there. The only place Horace will be racing is to the bottom of the sea!"

"Jimmy?" said Maverick desperately. "Jimmy, are you there?"

"Of course I am," said Jimmy.

"Oh, I thought you must have left and that some idiot had taken your place," said Maverick.

"What do you mean?" asked Jimmy in surprise.

"We can't send Horace down a hole in the ice!" cried Maverick. "That's exactly what he did to us, which was awful! It would make us just as bad as him."

"No, it wouldn't," said Jimmy fiercely. "We'd just be paying him back. He started it."

"And besides," said Maverick, "the robo-pummeler is for getting us through snowy roads, not for smashing through the ice and sending people to the bottom of the sea — even if it is smelly Horace Pelly."

"Listen, Maverick," said Jimmy. "If we can take Horace out of the race, we'll win for sure. And that robo-upgrade will be ours! Big Al wouldn't think twice about it. He'd be knocking a hole in the ice faster than Pete Webber can change a tire!"

"Yes, but —"

"Activating rocket-boosters," said Jimmy, stabbing a finger at a button.

A flash of flame sent them rocketing past Horace and skidding over the ice.

"Activating robo-pummeler," said Jimmy, pulling the orange lever forward.

"JIMMY —" Maverick yelled as he hopped across the ice, jumping up and down like a kangaroo, the robo-pummeler thumping and banging holes in the ice as they went.

In his rearview mirror, Jimmy grinned as he saw thick, black cracks ripping through the ice, rocketing toward Zoom like lightning bolts.

"Jimmy!" Maverick yelled frantically. "What have you done?"

CHAPTER 10
BACKFIRE

"Look!" cried Jimmy, glancing in Maverick's rearview mirror. Zoom was bumping and bouncing over the jigsaw of breaking ice.

The sound of cracking ice rang around the ice cliffs like gunfire. The cracks widened and filled with seawater. Steam poured from Zoom's trunk as he went into a total spin, hurtling away from Maverick in widening circles and careening toward a huge hole in the ice.

Jimmy swallowed hard as he watched Zoom reach the very edge of the ice, about to plunge into the freezing water. But with an enormous roar from Zoom's engine, Horace regained control and managed to pull back from the brink, steering his robot toward safer ground.

Jimmy suddenly felt a little uncomfortable. Thinking about teaching Horace a lesson was one thing, but actually doing it was another. He forced down the guilt that was building inside him and pressed the accelerator harder. In Maverick's rearview mirror, the image of Horace and Zoom got smaller and smaller until the two were out of sight.

Jimmy glanced at the radar screen. He could see the green blip that was Horace and Zoom. Around the edge of the screen, four other moving blips had appeared. Jimmy realized it was the other robots. They must be getting near the point where the tracks all met and the racers joined up again. The final stretch before the finish line!

"We're getting close to the end of the ice track, I think," said Jimmy. "And we've left Horace way behind!"

"Oh, good," said Maverick flatly. "And all we had to do was cheat. So that's great, isn't it?"

"What do you mean?" said Jimmy defensively. "I only did what any of the other racers would have done. And Big Al would definitely have done it," he added.

"Would he?" Maverick asked. "Have you ever seen him pull a stunt like that? And even if he would do it, the Jimmy Roberts I know wouldn't."

Jimmy said nothing. He stared grimly at the ice ahead and chewed angrily at his bottom lip. He glanced at Maverick's rearview mirror, half hoping to see Horace racing up behind them.

I might even let Horace overtake, Jimmy thought, *it would make me feel better about what I did.* There was still no sign of Horace in the mirror, but there was something shooting toward them.

In horror, Jimmy suddenly realized what it was. The cracks in the ice that Jimmy had started with the robo-pummeler were still spreading, and fast, chasing Maverick across the white surface like giant snakes.

"Maverick, the ice —" he screamed.

But it was too late. All around him, the ice began to crack.

"Hold on!" Jimmy shouted, veering left then right, then left again, trying to make his way across the collapsing ice. Every way he turned, the ice in front of them disappeared under the freezing sea, which welled up in its place. Ahead of them, another fracture appeared in the slippery white surface, and Jimmy had to slam on the brakes, screeching to a halt.

In stunned silence, Jimmy looked around him at the chaos he had created. For hundreds of feet in almost every direction, chunks of broken ice bobbed in the churning Arctic Ocean. He and Maverick were perched on a narrow stretch of ice like a finger pointing out from the solid ice shelf.

"Phew!" said Jimmy, getting his breath back. "That was a close one. Now that we're back on solid ground —"

"Solid ice," corrected Maverick.

"— we can get going again," finished Jimmy.

Maverick's engines roared to life once more,

but they sounded very strange. It was his normal engine noise but with strange creaking and groaning added.

"What is it?" asked Jimmy. "What's wrong?"

In dismay, Jimmy realized what was happening. The noise wasn't from Maverick's engines. It was the ice underneath them!

The creaking and groaning became an ear-splitting screech as the finger of ice they were on broke away from the main ice shelf.

"Quick, Maverick!" he cried. "We have to jump it!"

But it was too late. All they could do was sit and watch as they began to drift out into the Arctic Ocean.

CHAPTER 11
ALL AT SEA

For almost a minute, Jimmy sat perfectly still and silent. The only sound was of water lapping against the ice slab on which Maverick was floating. He looked back at the ice sheet they had left behind, and then stared out to sea. It stretched for miles and miles — all the way to the horizon and the gray sky, which they were slowly drifting toward.

Jimmy heard the whine of an engine in the distance. It grew louder and louder. Around a corner of the rapidly disappearing coastline came Princess Kako on Lightning, bouncing across the waves on her robobike-turned-jet-ski.

She weaved between the icebergs, throwing her weight expertly from side to side as she raced past.

With a jolt, Jimmy realized they must have floated into the sea track of the race! He hopped out of Maverick and ran to the edge of the iceberg.

"Hey, Kako! Kako! Hey!" he shouted. "Help!"

She didn't hear him. She didn't see him. Jimmy watched in dismay as the foaming trail she left behind was washed away by the waves. Kako disappeared beyond the ice cliffs.

A couple of seconds later, the huge hoverbot Maximus, piloted by Sammy, came roaring around the same corner. His dual air cushions glided effortlessly across the sea. His enormous propellers sent up waves, rocking Jimmy and Maverick's floating ice island.

Jimmy waved and jumped and shouted and finally came to a standstill as Sammy followed Kako and was gone.

"Ugh!" he yelled in frustration, stomping his foot on the hard white surface beneath his snow boot. Then he climbed back onboard Maverick and sank into his seat. "So," he said, "what do we do?"

Maverick said nothing.

"Maverick?" Jimmy asked.

Silence.

Jimmy pressed Maverick's engine starter. His engine leaped into life.

"Maverick?" Jimmy tried again. "Maverick?"

Nothing.

Panic made Jimmy's stomach churn. Maverick must have been damaged somehow.

"Say something, Maverick!" he said, pushing another button.

With the panic rushing up from his stomach to his throat, Jimmy pressed another button. Then another button. And another. Nothing worked.

Then suddenly the robot was back in action. Before Jimmy could do anything to stop him, Maverick threw himself into a doughnut — spinning in incredibly fast and tight little circles, flying around the ice slab with his emergency siren blaring. In panic, Jimmy stabbed at another button. It made Maverick go even faster. He pressed it again. Maverick went faster still. He pushed it once more — harder this time. Maverick's doors started slamming open and shut, open and shut again.

"Ugh!" Jimmy cried.

Maverick's doors flapped wildly. Then he was off again, reversing to the very edge of the ice slab, closer and closer to the water. Jimmy grabbed the steering wheel and yanked it straight.

"Brake!" yelped Maverick. Without thinking, Jimmy stomped on the brake pedal and they skidded to a standstill. Jimmy jumped out of Maverick as though the driver's seat was burning him. They were perched on the very edge of the ice slab with freezing seawater lapping at Maverick's front tires. Another inch and they would have been heading down to the bottom of the sea again.

"Maverick?" cried Jimmy. "Are you okay? What happened? Did you malfunction?"

"I don't have to talk all the time," said Maverick quietly. "Just because I don't feel like having a chat, there's no need to start prodding and pressing every button you can see."

"You didn't feel like talking to me?" repeated Jimmy. "I thought you were broken!"

"Well, maybe I don't feel like talking when you've stopped listening," said Maverick angrily. "It's a waste of my exhaust fumes, especially when your decisions leave us floating around the Arctic on a giant ice cube."

Jimmy looked at the robot, open-mouthed. A feeling of shame was slowly burning through him, making him want to run away and hide. He knew Grandpa wouldn't be proud of him for trying to sabotage another racer. And now even Maverick didn't want to know him.

He took a deep breath. "Maverick, I'm so sorry. I was being a complete idiot. I should have listened to you."

"I know," said Maverick.

"And I promise not to ignore you from now on," said Jimmy.

"Good," said Maverick.

"So do you forgive me? Are we friends again?"

Maverick said nothing.

"Please?" said Jimmy.

"Of course," said Maverick. "Apology accepted."

Jimmy grinned in relief.

"So how do we get off this ice cube and back in the race?" Maverick continued. "We need a plan."

"Okay," said Jimmy. "We could . . ." He paused. Ten seconds passed, and still he couldn't think of a good idea. Ten seconds turned to twenty seconds. Then he said, "I know! I'll give you a quick tune-up."

"How's that going to get us back on dry land?" Maverick asked.

"It's not," Jimmy replied, "but I might as well do something useful while I'm thinking of a way to get off this icicle and back in the race."

"Good idea," said Maverick, "and I think I might have a quick reboot and self-repair. My sensors are feeling a little scrambled. I'll go quiet for a minute, but I'll be back before you know it. Don't push any more buttons."

Jimmy hurried to Maverick's trunk and got out the toolkit that Pete Webber had lent him. Also in the trunk was a fruit and veggie box from That's Shallot! that Jimmy had completely forgotten about. The contents were frozen solid, but that didn't stop him from popping a couple of raspberries into his mouth.

Jimmy had a quick look under the hood and cleaned Maverick's firing mechanism; checked his coolant, oil, brake fluid; and tightened his tire bolts. By the time he finished, Maverick had rebooted.

"Ahhh," sighed Maverick, "that's much better. Everything's peachy. I've even managed to get Cabcom back online. Got a plan yet?"

"Not exactly," said Jimmy.

"Not exactly? Or not at all?" asked Maverick.

Jimmy sighed in frustration. "If only you could turn into a jet ski like Lightning," he grumbled.

"Well," snapped Maverick, "I'm so sorry to let you down."

"Or if you had a propeller like Maximus does, we could —"

Jimmy stopped talking. His mood lifted as he had a sudden thought.

"What?" said Maverick. "What is it?"

"The propeller thing!" cried Jimmy.

"What propeller thing?" asked Maverick.

"Your propeller thing!" said Jimmy.

"I don't have a propeller thing," said Maverick.

"No, the thing Pete put in," explained Jimmy excitedly. "Spins around . . . cuts through stuff. You know!"

"Do you mean the roto-blade?" asked Maverick.

"That's it!" said Jimmy. "Maverick, we're going to turn this ice cube into a motorboat!"

CHAPTER 12
SAILING THROUGH

"I hope no one can see us," muttered Maverick. "This is so embarrassing."

Maverick was parked with his trunk open at the very edge of the ice slab. He had extended the roto-blade on its long steel arm. With a little help from a wrench taken from Pete Webber's toolkit, Jimmy had managed to adjust the angle of the arm and bend it downward so that the blade's long, razor-sharp teeth were under the water.

From a distance, came a whirring that sounded like a swarm of flies. Out of the gray cloud flew two of the camerabots that filmed the races for television. As they got nearer, they slowed and hovered, one directly overhead, the other a little farther away.

"Great," muttered Maverick. "How many people are watching us live on TV while I've got my bum in the air?"

"Millions," said Jimmy, trying not to laugh. "So we'd better make sure this works."

"No pressure then," muttered Maverick.

"Ready?" asked Jimmy. He jumped into Maverick's cockpit and pushed the roto-blade button. Its motor sprang into life, and from beneath the water came the whir of the blade and a rush of froth and bubbles.

"Are we moving?" called Jimmy.

"Yes!" cried Maverick. "Yes! We're moving!" And then he went quiet. "Sensors indicate our current speed is approximately . . . two miles per hour. Traveling at this speed, we should complete the race by Tuesday next week."

"It's working!" said Jimmy. "But not well enough. Adjust the angle on the blade, Maverick."

Maverick lifted the roto-blade out of the water, lengthened the arm a little, and lowered it back into the water.

"How's that?" he asked.

"I think we're going faster!" cried Jimmy.

"Six miles an hour," said Maverick. "No! Ten . . . fifteen . . . twenty! Twenty-five miles an hour and rising!"

Jimmy grinned. "It works!" he cheered.

Little by little, they picked up more speed, and soon they were cruising smoothly between the chunks of floating ice and heading back toward the ice shelf.

"Left a little . . . right a little," Jimmy called. "Can we go any faster?"

"Hang on," said Maverick, increasing the revs on the roto-blade. "How's that?"

With a surge and a wash of foam and spray, the ice boat shot forward.

"This is incredible!" shouted Jimmy. "We should have thought of this before!"

"I hope those camerabots are getting some good shots," said Maverick.

"Can you get Robo TV working again so we can see?" said Jimmy.

"I'll give it a try," replied the robot. "The electronics should all be dry and warm again."

There was a clicking noise, and then the screen on Cabcom flickered to life.

". . . something we've never seen before in the history of Robot Races," one of the TV commentators was saying. "Incredible!" The pictures showed an aerial shot of Maverick and Jimmy racing over the waves leaving a trail of foam behind them. Jimmy looked up and waved at the camerabot. "And hi to you too, Jimmy Roberts," said the commentator, chuckling.

"There's no time for waving at the cameras," came Grandpa's voice — his face popping up on the Cabcom screen too. "You're coming up to the crossroads where the three tracks join up again. The track gets pretty narrow after it, so whoever gets there first has a huge advantage. Me and Pete were wondering where you'd gone to," he added, "but I love the speedboat. Great thinking, Jimmy boy!"

Jimmy smiled proudly . . . but not for long. Just then, a familiar black shape sped past on the ice track. Horace and Zoom had overtaken them again.

"No time to worry about them now," said Maverick. "It's time to get back on the ice." He adjusted the roto-blade and steered them toward the ice shelf.

They were heading for the solid ice at an alarming speed — but not fast enough.

Jimmy realized they needed to time their landing perfectly if they were going to avoid getting wet for the second time that day.

"Okay," he said, trying not to sound worried. "Retract roto-blade, Maverick. We want to glide off this ice cube and back onto the ice shelf. If we hit it too hard, we'll smash the ice and end up at the bottom of the sea."

The ice shelf got nearer. From the water, the ice looked incredibly thick — like a huge step with which they were about to collide. It was going to be a bumpy ride.

"Ready to go?" asked Jimmy.

"Ready," said Maverick. "Get your driving head on!"

Jimmy climbed into Maverick's cockpit. As they neared the ice shelf, Maverick's engine roared and Jimmy's foot hovered over the accelerator.

"Ten feet," said Maverick in quiet concentration. "Five feet . . ." Jimmy put Maverick into gear. "Three feet . . . Go! GO! GO!"

Jimmy slammed his foot on the pedal just as they hit the ice shelf with a terrific thump. In a cloud of smoke, Maverick flew off the ice raft and hit the ice with a massive, bone-shaking, brain-rattling thud. In one smooth sweep of the wheel, Jimmy guided Maverick back onto the racetrack and headed for the crossroads where all three routes joined up once again.

"Awesome!" said Maverick.

"Not bad," agreed Jimmy with a modest smile.

"Jimmy!" called Maverick. "Look at the radar."

Jimmy looked.

The radar's green glowing line swept around the screen, but where there had earlier been five blinking dots, now there was just one big blob.

"Who is it?" he asked. "Has the radar gone haywire?"

"I don't know," said Maverick. "My navigation says we're on track, and my sensors show all of the other racers are nearby."

"What does it mean?"

"I don't know," said Maverick.

They could make out a deep rumbling sound like the noise an airplane made at takeoff. And then, as they rounded a bend in the track they saw a sight that made Jimmy gasp. "Maverick, look!"

The track up ahead followed the shape of the coastline, with the ocean on the left and a cliff face towering over it on the right — a monstrous, snow-capped glacier. Part of the snow cliff had broken away and fallen onto the track! As they watched, more snow came tumbling down, bouncing off the jagged hillside.

Tons and tons of snow cascaded down like a frosty waterfall.

After a few seconds, the avalanche eased and the rumbling of falling snow faded to an echo. As the powdery fog cleared, Jimmy could just make out five shapes sticking out of the snow. It was the other racers, in a massive, icy pileup!

CHAPTER 13
PILEUP

As Jimmy carefully drove Maverick closer, he realized what had happened. Missy must have grazed the sides of the glacier with Monster's huge tires and caused the avalanche. Now Monster was almost completely buried in deep, deep snow.

Behind Monster was Dug — at least, Jimmy thought it was Dug. All he could see was a digger arm poking out of a mountain of fallen snow. Dug was followed by Maximus, Lightning, and Zoom. They had all been almost completely buried, and they were truly stuck.

It was chaos. Complete chaos.

"This is our chance," Maverick said excitedly. "We just need to get past them, and we'll be on that winner's podium for sure!"

"But how are we going to get through?" Jimmy asked.

"The robo-pummeler," Maverick replied without hesitation. "It looks like there's a way through down the left-hand side of the pileup, but we'll need to compact that snow so that I don't get stuck like the rest of them. And we don't want to slip and fall back into the sea. I've had enough of that for one day."

"Right," Jimmy said. "That special prize has got our name on it —"

But before Jimmy could finish speaking, there was another rumble, and the cliff face above the robots began to move. Jimmy could see it slowly shifting.

"That doesn't sound good," Jimmy said. "Look at that!" Jimmy pointed to the top of the cliff, where a big crack was appearing in the cliff.

It wasn't snow coming loose now — it was a giant block of ice!

"That's got to be as big as a house," Jimmy said, biting his lip. "If that comes down, it'll squash them all like pancakes! Maverick, we have to do something!"

"But I thought you would do anything to win?" Maverick said. "What does it matter what happens to them as long as we beat them? Besides, the safetybots will be here soon enough. Let's go!"

Jimmy stomped on the brakes. "I've learned my lesson, Maverick. It's not worth winning if you have to hurt everyone else to do it. I'm not Horace Pelly."

Maverick's headlights blinked happily. "Well said, Jimmy buddy."

Then there was a flash of orange from deep within the snowdrift, followed by even more groaning from the cliff face.

"Horace is trying to burn his way out with that flamethrower of his," said Maverick. "That kind of heat will make the cliff even less stable."

At that moment, a new face appeared on the Cabcom. It was Lord Leadpipe, and he didn't look well. The multi-billionaire's face was pale, and he looked like he had seen a ghost. "Calling all racers, calling all racers," he said. "We're having a . . . um . . . ah . . . slight technical hitch with the safetybots. It appears there's been a malfunction with their deicers, so they've all frozen solid."

He coughed nervously, and then tried to put a smile on his face. It looked more like a grimace to Jimmy. "If you children could, um, keep out of trouble while we sort out the problem, then I'll have them up and running in just a jiffy." And with that, his face disappeared and the screen went blank.

"No one's coming to the rescue," Jimmy gasped. "We have to do something!"

"Aye, aye, Captain!" Maverick said, revving his engine.

"Can you turn on Cabcom?" said Jimmy. "I need to talk to everyone."

Cabcom crackled into life.

"Did you hear Lord Leadpipe?" asked Jimmy. "The safetybots aren't coming. It's up to us to get out of this. But everyone needs to help. Okay?"

Horace's face popped up on the screen. "I suppose you can't make things any worse," he said with a sneer.

Jimmy ignored him. "I'm going to dig you all out using my roto-blade, but everyone will have to be very careful. There's a big slab of ice coming loose at the top of the cliff, and any loud noises or sudden movements might cause an avalanche."

"Thanks, Jimmy," said Kako.

"Great," said Sammy.

"We're relying on ya, buddy," said Chip.

"Cheers, mate!" bellowed Missy.

"Well, go on then," said Horace.

The screen went blank again.

"Activate roto-blade?" said Maverick.

"Yeah, but easy does it, Maverick," said Jimmy.

Maverick extended the roto-blade on its long steel arm. Like a dentist performing surgery on a tooth, they carefully cut through the white snow. Jimmy edged Maverick forward inch by inch, his nerves trembling as he listened carefully for any sound of another avalanche.

It took just a couple of minutes to get Horace free. In a shower of white dust, the metal blades cut into the snowdrift, scattering it into the Arctic wind.

"Careful of Zoom's bodywork. It's custom painted," came Horace's voice from the Cabcom. "If you damage it, you'll have to pay."

"I think you mean 'thank you for rescuing us'!" Maverick snapped.

"All right, Horace," Jimmy began, "I need you to help me get Lightning and Maximus free now. Can you just —"

Jimmy didn't get a chance to finish. Horace had fired up Zoom's engines and was revving them loudly.

"Horace, what are you doing?" shouted Jimmy into Cabcom.

Horace didn't reply. He was too busy activating Zoom's rocket-boosters. Before anyone could say anything, huge tongues of fire shot from Zoom's exhaust. He shot up the snowdrift where the others were trapped and skated over the top.

"Ha!" Horace yelled triumphantly as he and Zoom landed safely on the other side. "Later, losers." And without another word, he disappeared in the direction of the finish line.

A second or two passed while Jimmy stared open-mouthed at the blank screen. He couldn't believe what Horace had just done. "What an idiot!" he said.

"Yup," said Maverick.

Cabcom leaped back into life, and Missy's face appeared, looking red and anxious.

"I don't want to worry you guys," she whispered, "but the ice up where I am is making some pretty strange noises. I think Horace and his rocket-boosters have done it some damage and —"

A deep cracking sound in the ice above them cut Missy off. Jimmy glanced out of Maverick's window. A huge crack was spreading way above their heads, and lumps of ice and snow began to rain down on them. A second cracking sound rang out, and the ice cliff shook. As the ice shifted, a chunk the size of a car broke off and fell toward the remaining racers.

Jimmy looked at it in horror. The sky went dark as the ice block's shadow fell across them.

BOOM!

The slab hit the track and exploded into a million pieces, no more than a few feet from where Kako and Lightning were half buried. Shards of ice were fired in every direction.

Then there was silence.

Jimmy let out a long, slow breath. "That was close," he whispered.

"Yep," Maverick agreed. "And the rest could come down on us all at any minute!"

CHAPTER 14
CLIFFHANGER

Jimmy and Maverick had just finished chipping away the last of the snow surrounding Kako and Lightning when a light started flashing on Cabcom.

"There's a message coming through from Chip," said Maverick.

Jimmy flicked a switch, and Chip's face filled the screen. "Calling all racers," he whispered. "I don't know about the rest of y'all, but I wanna get out of this mess right about now."

There was a muttering of agreement from the others. They were all a little shaken up by the explosion.

Jimmy sat in complete silence for a few seconds. "We need a better plan," he whispered finally to Maverick. "What do you think?"

"Well," said Maverick, "we could race up the snowdrift, over the tops of Dug and Missy and head for the finish line . . ."

"Like Horace did?"

"Yup," said Maverick. "Or we could stay here and help the others get out of this mess."

"We have to stay and help," Jimmy said firmly. "And there's no time to lose," he continued as another shower of ice rained down on them from the glacier. Jimmy leaned into the Cabcom. "Sammy, I'm using my roto-blade to clear the snow around you next. Okay?"

"No, Jimmy, not okay," Sammy replied, his anxious face staring out from the Cabcom screen. "Your blades will puncture my air cushions for certain. Maximus will be stuck here, and we'll be blocking everyone else in. I'm thinking we should try a different way."

"Okay," said Jimmy. "Maverick, switch all systems to manual. I'm taking over."

"What?" said Maverick.

"I'm taking responsibility for this," said Jimmy, "so if it all goes wrong, it's my fault."

"Okay, Jimmy boy," Maverick said. "You've listened to me, now I'll listen to you. We're a team. But be careful," he added nervously.

Jimmy pressed a button on the steering wheel, and a compartment on Maverick's hood slid open. Up rose the grappling hooks, the sharpened points glinting in the light. Jimmy prodded another button, and the angle of the grappling hooks lowered by a few degrees.

"A little more," said Jimmy. "And a little more . . ."

Cabcom crackled. Sammy's face appeared, red and angry. "What are you doing? You're aiming straight at Maximus! You'll hit him!"

"Trust me, Sammy. I know what I'm doing. Fire!" said Jimmy, pushing the button.

The grappling hook flew at Maximus, missed his rear left propeller by about an inch, and crashed into the ice cliff. It bounced off and sent a shower of ice chips over Maximus's cab.

"Jimmy, stop right now!" Sammy shouted.

Jimmy leaned over to the screen and turned it off. Then he reeled the grappling hook back in on its thick steel cable. It clattered and clanked over the ice, making its way back to the launcher on Maverick's hood. "I'm reloading and adjusting the angle," he said determinedly. "Two inches right."

He paused and took a deep breath.

"Here goes!" He pushed the launch button again. This time the grappling hook flew between Maximus's propellers and wrapped itself around the steel structure on which his propellers were mounted.

"Yes!" shouted Jimmy. "Gotcha. Reel him in, Maverick. We'll drag Maximus out of the snow. Once he's free, he can help us dig the others out."

"Amazing!" Maverick cried. "But . . . how . . . I mean . . ." he stuttered.

"Has your speech software malfunctioned?" Jimmy said. "Just keep your circuits crossed that this works, otherwise we're all in big trouble."

The steel cable dragged Maverick forward, making him slip awkwardly on the ice.

"We need to anchor ourselves, Maverick," said Jimmy. "Otherwise we'll end up stuck in there too."

"I've got just the thing," replied the robot. "You aren't the only one with a few tricks up his sleeve valve."

Clunk!

Two sharpened pieces of metal, shaped like skewers, thudded into the ground and secured Maverick firmly in place.

"Ready?" Jimmy asked.

"Ready," said Maverick.

Jimmy pressed the winch button again. It took less than thirty seconds to drag Sammy free. "Yes!" shouted Maverick. "We did it!"

The screen on Cabcom lit up to show that Sammy was trying to make another call, and this time Jimmy answered it.

Sammy's smiling face appeared. "Jimmy, Maverick, thank you," said Sammy. "I should have trusted you."

"No problem," said Jimmy. "Now we need to help the other two and then get ourselves out of here. That block of ice could come toppling down any moment."

With Maximus and Lightning now free, there was more room to maneuver. Next came Dug and Chip. The combined efforts of Maverick's roto-blade with Dug's own dextrous arm with a scoop on the end helped them to make short work of getting the digger-bot free.

That just left Missy and Monster trapped.

They had almost forgotten about the danger they were in when an ear-splitting crack echoed overhead. Jimmy looked up to see a six-foot dagger of ice hurtling down toward them.

"Look out!" he yelled into the Cabcom at the top of his lungs. All of the freed racers took evasive action, moving out of the way just in time as the icicle struck the ground where they had just been, shattering into a thousand tiny pieces.

"That was awful close," came Chip's voice over the Cabcom. "Looks like we're going to need to work faster and quieter, y'all. So let's get this thing done."

Without another word, and with their power as low as they could, Maverick, Dug, and Lightning circled Monster, digging and plowing and chipping her free from the snow.

"If we can just shift a little more of this snow, Monster should be able to pull herself out," said Jimmy. "Come on, Maverick. We need to get this done before that ice comes crashing down."

"How's it looking, Missy?" whispered Jimmy into Cabcom.

"Good," mumbled Missy. Jimmy could tell she was doing her best to talk quietly, something that was hard for the larger-than-life Australian girl. "Another couple of minutes and I should be clear," she said.

The glacier creaked above them. Another six-foot ice spear dropped, landing in a snowdrift just a few inches from Lightning.

"Fire up your engines, Missy," gasped Jimmy. "I don't think we have another couple of minutes. You need to try to pull yourself out right now."

Before Jimmy had even turned Cabcom off, Monster's engines roared into life. The tops of her huge tires started turning, sliding, and edging forward. Then they started rolling backward as they slid against the wall of snow and ice around them.

"Come on," muttered Jimmy to himself through clenched teeth.

Again, Missy opened up Monster's throttle and battered against the snow. She climbed up about a foot and almost made it out onto the flat, but slipped and rolled back again.

"Come on," hissed Jimmy again, sweat trickling down the back of his neck.

"Almost there," came Missy's voice over Cabcom, just as a deafening rumble came from the glacier.

Up came Monster again, pushing up and out of the snow — and suddenly she was free!

"Quickly, everyone," he yelled into Cabcom. "Let's go, go, go!"

There was a roar of engines. They were all past worrying about making too much noise. Missy and Monster lurched forward. They were closely followed by Maximus and Sammy, Lightning and Kako, Dug and Chip, and lastly, Jimmy and Maverick.

"It's breaking off!" Maverick shouted. The house-sized block of ice slid from its perch at the top of the glacier and fell over the edge.

There was a whistling sound as it sliced through the air and fell down, down, down — right toward Jimmy and Maverick.

"Aaaaaaahhhh!" Jimmy yelled as his foot squashed the accelerator. "Go, Maverick!"

Maverick was tossed into the air by the shock waves as the ice block smashed through the track just a few feet behind them. He skidded as he landed, his tires screeching in protest. For a moment, Jimmy thought he would swerve straight back into the ocean, but he managed to catch the slide and steer Maverick back to the center of the track. Only then did he dare look in his rearview mirror.

It looked like something out of a disaster movie. The whole section of track had disappeared behind them, and the icy surface had been smashed into little pieces that fizzed and frothed in the ocean.

"We did it, Maverick!" Jimmy cheered.

"And just in time," the robot replied.

"A marvelous effort, my boy, marvelous!" said Grandpa. "See you at the finish line."

The Cabcom went silent.

"Well," said Maverick, "you had me worried for a minute back there."

"Me too," said Jimmy. "But we don't have any time to waste. There's still a race to be won and not much time to do it."

"No problem, Jimmy. I'll shift all power to the engines, and we'll be right back in this r—" Maverick suddenly went silent.

CHAPTER 15
LAST

"What's the matter, Maverick," Jimmy asked, looking worried.

"I've got some bad news," the robot said. "I've just detected a puncture in my back tire."

"What happened? Can we fix it?" Jimmy asked. He had a sick feeling in his stomach, like he had eaten a whole carton of rotten eggs.

"Normally, yes. Your grandpa fitted an automatic reinflation device, but I can't work it. There's an icicle stuck in the tire. In fact, it pierced all the way through to the wheel."

Jimmy was silent for a second. Then he said, "So what now?"

"We'll just have to limp to the finish," Maverick said. "Sorry, Jimmy."

Jimmy jammed his foot down on the accelerator a little harder. The steering wheel squirmed in his hands as the flat tire wobbled dangerously. The finish line was so close that he could almost touch it, but there was nothing else they could do but watch through the zoom screen as the others finished the race. He thumped the steering wheel in frustration. "Of all the reasons for losing a race . . . a flat tire!"

Up ahead, Missy and Monster were barging past Chip and Dug, who then pushed their way back to the front again, almost sending Kako and Lightning off the ice track and into the snowdrifts. Maximus followed, swerving left and right, trying to find a way through.

He sighed as he saw Monster and Missy racing over the finish line. Chip and Dug followed soon after, then Kako on Lightning, and just behind them, Sammy and Maximus. But Horace had finished long before them all. He was already out of Zoom, leaning on the hood of his robot with a huge smirk on his face. Jimmy thought about the zero points he would get for finishing last, and felt a lump in his throat.

I could have won this race so easily, he thought. *But then, what would have happened to the others?*

"Never mind, Jimmy," said Maverick, as if he had read Jimmy's thoughts. "The important thing is that you did the right thing. I bet there's never been a robot racer who's done something more selfless than what you did today."

"Thanks, Maverick. There's always next time," Jimmy murmured as they crossed the finish line in last place.

"Sorry, Jimmy," said Maverick. "I did my best."

Tired and disappointed, Jimmy climbed out of Maverick's cockpit. Slowly he raised his head to the big screens hanging from the grandstands on either side. Each of the giant TVs showed the image of him stood, next to Maverick. Strange. The camerabots are always focused on the winner after the races.

But as he slowly took in the scene within the finish line area, he couldn't help but notice that every lens was focused on him. And every steward, mechanic, and race official was clapping and cheering him.

Then he heard the commentator yelling over the noise, "Ladies and gentlemen, I give you the hero of the race . . . Jimmy Roberts!"

Jimmy couldn't help but grin. He gave a little wave and a shy smile to the camera before slowly making his way to where the other racers had gathered. *Maybe winning isn't everything after all,* he thought.

Just then Jimmy caught sight of the one person he didn't want to see. Horace Pelly was wandering over to him, a broad smile of triumph on his smug face.

"I was wondering where you all had gone to," said Horace. "I came across the finish line about twenty minutes ago. If I'm not mistaken, that makes me the winner of an amazing Leadpipe Industries upgrade! Not that I'm surprised."

Jimmy, Princess Kako, Missy, Chip, and Sammy formed a circle around Horace and were staring angrily at him.

"What's wrong?" asked Horace.

"What's wrong?" bellowed Missy in disbelief.

"Yes, you won this race, Horace," said Sammy, "but do you know what danger you caused the rest of us?"

"I can't help it if you losers get yourselves stuck, can I?" Horace said. He smirked at them.

"But you sure didn't need to put us all in danger, did you, mate? That stunt of yours could have brought down the whole glacier!" bellowed Missy. "You're as dumb as they come, Horace Pelly. You should be ashamed of yourself."

"We could all have been killed out there today if it hadn't been for Jimmy," Chip added.

"Let's not get carried away," said Horace. "Jimmy's not perfect. You should have seen the stunt he pulled on me earlier in the race. It was just as bad."

Jimmy felt a burst of shame. He stepped forward in front of everyone and looked at

Horace. "I'm really, really sorry about that. I'll never do anything like that again."

"Whatever, loser," he said.

Joshua Johnson, the Robot Coordinator, appeared on the other side of the pit area. He was waving his clipboard urgently. "Horace, if you could stop chatting and come to the winners' podium, please? And Missy and Chip? Could you come too, please?"

"Hear that, Jimmy?" Horace grinned. "The winners' podium. That would be the podium for winners. Not losers like you."

As they made their way over to the awards ceremony, Lord Leadpipe stood at the podium with a microphone.

"In third place with six points," he said, "Chip Travers and Dug."

"In second place for eight points," continued Lord Leadpipe, "Missy McGovern and Monster."

"And in first place, taking the ten points," said Lord Leadpipe, "Horace Pelly and Zoom."

Horace stepped up onto the podium with his hands in the air, waving at the camerabots. But

the atmosphere had suddenly gone flat. Jimmy
thought he might even have heard one or two
people booing. Horace didn't seem to notice. He
grinned with his huge white teeth and winked
at the cameras. Then he turned to face Lord
Leadpipe expectantly.

"And as the winner of the Arctic Adventure,
Horace," continued Lord Leadpipe, "I am
particularly proud to present you with a very
special prize from Leadpipe Industries."

Horace's face lit up. Lord Leadpipe beckoned
to Joshua Johnson, who climbed onto the
podium holding something covered in purple
cloth. Horace held out his hands in expectation.
Lord Leadpipe took hold of the cloth and
whisked it away like a magician revealing a dove
in a cage. But it wasn't a dove in a cage. Joshua
was holding a red velvet cushion with an object
resting on it. Lord Leadpipe lifted the object
from the cushion and ceremoniously handed it
to Horace. The crowd fell silent.

"This," said Lord Leadpipe, "I am very
proud to say, has been specially created

to commemorate fifty years of Leadpipe Industries." He handed it to Horace.

Horace stared at it for a moment. "What is it?" he demanded.

"That," said Lord Leadpipe, "is a piece of lead pipe, taken from the very first processing plant where I began —"

"A piece of pipe?" repeated Horace in disbelief. "Made of lead?"

"You must be very proud," said Lord Leadpipe.

Jimmy could see Missy trying to hide a smile. "It's just part of an old pipe," she mouthed, stifling a giggle. Sammy snorted with laughter, but managed to cover it up as a cough. And Chip was grinning broadly. They all knew how much Horace had wanted a fancy upgrade — and how much he would have gloated about using it in the next race. Even the quiet and usually straight-faced Kako broke into a smile.

Sensing an outburst from Horace at any moment, Joshua Johnson hurriedly hustled him and Lord Leadpipe from the podium.

As the ceremony came to a close, Jimmy spotted Grandpa. He ran to give him a hug.

"Did you see Horace, Grandpa?"

Grandpa nodded and smiled. "I did, my boy. I don't think that Horace Pelly really understands sentimental value, does he?"

"It doesn't look like it," Jimmy replied.

"Anyway, I'm proud of you, boy," said Grandpa as they headed back to Maverick. "You didn't win this one, but you showed enough courage for ten robot racers."

"Thanks, Grandpa," said Jimmy, his smile glowing with happiness.

"And," continued Grandpa, "you're still at the top of the leader board, tied with young Chip at eighteen points. It's getting tight with that good-for-nothing Horace Pelly just behind you at sixteen points, along with Princess Kako. Then it's Missy at fourteen points and Sammy at twelve."

That made Jimmy feel even better. He had just had his worst race yet, but he still had a shot.

"That was an incredible race," said Pete as he came walking over. "You made a big mistake with that robo-pummeler, but — you know what? — Big Al sometimes gets carried away like that. He can't think about anything but winning. But like you, he always does the right thing in the end," he nodded.

"Thanks, Pete," said Jimmy, his cheeks burning with pride. He loved it when Pete compared him to Big Al. "Will you be back working with us for the next race?" he asked.

"Don't know," growled Pete. "I'll have to talk to Lord Leadpipe and see what he —"

"Did I hear my name?" said Lord Leadpipe, strolling over to them. "Something about Pete helping you with Maverick?" he said. "Well," he went on, putting an arm around Jimmy, "I can't tell you how proud I am of you, Jimmy. You were immensely brave in helping your fellow competitors. I would never have forgiven myself if something had happened today."

Jimmy could see that the billionaire was being deadly serious.

"I can't say I've ever seen anyone risk so much, sacrificing his own chances to protect others," Lord Leadpipe went on. A smile crept onto his face as he continued, "And bravery of that kind certainly deserves some kind of reward. Sadly, I can't bend the rules and give you the points you deserve. So I think the least we can do is lend you Pete Webber for a couple of weeks. If that's okay with you, Pete?"

"It sure is," said Pete.

"And would that be agreeable to you, Wilfred?" asked Lord Leadpipe.

Grandpa, who had been quietly staring at the ground since Lord Leadpipe appeared, looked up and smiled. "Of course!" he exclaimed. "You're welcome anytime, Pete. The kettle's always on!"

"You mean —" began Jimmy, who had finally managed to open his mouth and speak. "— you mean Pete Webber — *the* Pete Webber — is going to be working with us for two whole weeks?"

"If it's okay with you, Jimmy?" Pete asked as he smiled at Jimmy.

"Okay?" cried Jimmy. "Okay? It's more than okay. It's . . . amaaaazing!"

Pete laughed and patted him on the back.

"Oh, and one more thing," said Lord Leadpipe, leaning in. "There was a second special prize today, but seeing as my first offering was received with so little enthusiasm, I think it needs a different home. I think it should go to the hero of the race. Here you go." And with a wink he passed a small box to Jimmy.

Jimmy stood rooted to the spot. What could this package be?

"Open it, my dear boy. We don't have all day," Lord Leadpipe encouraged him.

"Go ahead, Jimmy. Open it," Grandpa said.

Carefully, Jimmy unwrapped the package to see a fat metal tube.

Pete's mouth dropped open as he looked at it. "Is that . . . ?"

"A sonic-booster," Leadpipe said proudly.

"Maverick's going to love it," Jimmy grinned. "Thank you! I don't know what to say. This is incredible!"

"There's nothing to say, Jimmy. You deserve it more than anybody . . . as you will see from the inscription on the side."

Jimmy turned the booster over and read the engraving out loud: "For a true racing spirit."

Lord Leadpipe grinned at Grandpa. And for once, Grandpa smiled back at him.

"That's quite some grandson you have, Wilfred," Lord Leadpipe said. "He's got a lot of fans rooting for him now, I believe. I expect a good performance next time you're on the track, Jimmy."

"Oh, don't you worry about that," replied Grandpa. "We will be ready to handle whatever you throw at us, won't we, my boy?"

"Of course we will," said Jimmy. "We've still got a championship to win!"